'Do you know what would be lovely,' Mum says in this stern, straight voice, 'would be if you could just come outdoors and not be dramatic for once.'

I scowl, folding my arms and crossing my brows. 'I can definitely do that, easy peasy lemon squeezy. I bet I CAN go a LIFETIME without making any drama AT ALL. I bet I can at LEAST do the whole entire six-week summer holidays. Without making one bit of drama about ANYTHING!'

'We'll see about that,' Mum taunts me.

'Oh, yes we will.'

Author and illustrator Laura Dockrill is a graduate of the BRIT School of Performing Arts and has appeared at many festival and literary events across the country, including the Edinburgh Fringe, Camp Bestival, Latitude and the Southbank Centre's Imagine Festival. Named one of the top ten literary talents by *The Times* and one of the top twenty hot faces to watch by *ELLE* magazine, she has performed her work on all the BBC's radio channels, including Gemma Cairney's Radio 1 show, plus appearances on Huw Murray, Colin Murray and Radio 4's *Woman's Hour*. In 2013 Laura was the Booktrust Online Writer in Residence and was named as a Guardian Culture Professionals Network 'Innovator, Visionary, Pioneer'. Laura has been a roving reporter for the Roald Dahl Funny Prize, and is on the advisory panel at the Ministry of Stories. The first *Darcy Burdock* book was shortlisted for the Waterstones Children's Book Prize 2014. She lives in south London with her bearded husband.

The *Darcy Burdock* series is Laura's first writing for children. After having her stage invaded by fifty rampaging kids during a reading of her work for adults at Camp Bestival, she decided she really enjoyed the experience and would very much like it to happen again. Laura would like to make it clear that any resemblance between herself-as-a-child and Darcy is entirely accurate.

'Everyone's falling for Laura Dockrill' – VOGUE

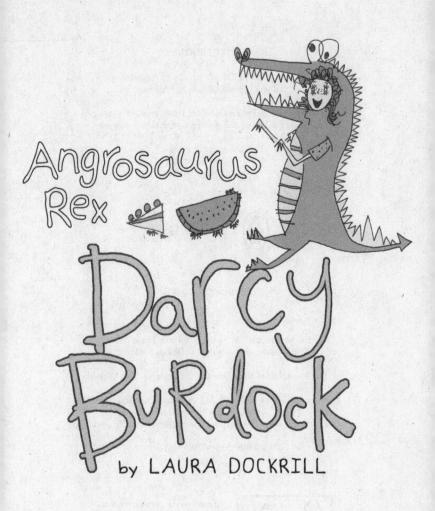

Angrosaurus Rex

Darcy Burdock

by LAURA DOCKRILL

CORGI BOOKS

CORGI BOOKS

UK | USA | Canada | Ireland | Australia
India | New Zealand | South Africa

Corgi Books is part of the Penguin Random House group of companies whose
addresses can be found at global.penguinrandomhouse.com.

www.penguin.co.uk
www.puffin.co.uk
www.ladybird.co.uk

Penguin
Random House
UK

First published 2017

001

Text and illustrations copyright © Laura Dockrill, 2017
Author photograph copyright © Dhillon Shukla, 2013

The moral right of the author and illustrator has been asserted.

Typeset in 12.5/15pt Baskerville MT by Falcon Oast Graphic Art Ltd
Printed in Great Britain by Clays Ltd, St Ives plc
A CIP catalogue record for this book is available from the British Library.

ISBN: 978-0-552-57255-2

For Kai, Kelda and Ilka

Chapter One

HOW ARE YOU GOING TO SPEND YOUR
SUMMER HOLIDAYS?

are the words written in massive letters on the board
in the big hall.

BLEUGH.

This is the head of year, Mrs Hay's, idea of a fun
way to break up for the six-week summer holidays. I
think she's probably devastated that she won't be
teaching me any more next year because we will be
moving up to Year Eight and getting a new head of
year. I am her most main wingman, so I have to be
very sensitive and patient to this activity she wants us

to do. She'll be relying on me, no doubt, to take it very seriously. Mr Yates, our actual class teacher, is finding the whole thing very amusing. Folding his arms, probably thinking to himself, *I have the best class in the whole school.* Which is accurate.

We basically, one at a time, have to stand up and take turns to tell everybody what 'we are going to do' in the summer holidays.

It's mostly sucker-upperers, people in my form class lying their fat heads off about how they are going to 'work on their spelling' or 'learn the flute' or 'help the elderly'.

But I am NOT buying it.

'I'm going to Spain and I'm gonna learn how to do a Superman – one of my cousins is going to teach me!' my best friend Will says.

'A Superman?' Mrs Hay lisps. Mrs Hay has old blonde hair – sprayed hair that is stuck into a frozed position like the top of an

2

ice cream – and she's really tall, and all her clothes and knowledge of the world is from the *complete* past. But she's nice. Her voice sounds like the brushing noise of tinsel. I try and ignore the fact that Will is going to be away. It's putting me in a right bad mood.

'It's a BMX trick, where you jump in the air but are only holding onto the handlebars, so you look like you're flying through the sky like Superman.'

Mrs Hay looks horrified. 'On a *bike*?' she spits. 'Why would you want to do that?'

'Cos it's fun!' Will shrieks. He then goes on to do an impression of 'the Superman', and everybody laughs. Mrs Hay even cracks a smile but that's probs because in ten minutes she can go relax and forget about us for six whole weeks.

'Darcy, you're up next. What are you going to do in the holidays?'

The eyes of my year group ping back at me. I really need to go out with a BANG of seeming cool and interesting.

'Probably just the usual,' I say. 'You know, great

and well-deserved relaxing weeks stuffed full to the brim with wild crazy circus trips and parties and sunny beaches of paradise and wandering through the woods and treasure hunts and sleeping in till lunch time and boat trips and theme parks and going to probably the opera – maybe even – and train journeys and getting to be a queen or be a wrestler or be an ape or be anything I wish! And movie jim-jam days and baking a cake and going to water parks, and then maybe I'll swing by Hawaii for *my* six-week holiday and wear a grass skirt and learn to hula with a bajillion multi-coloured flowers in my hair. Just being alive; BLISS!'

'Whoa! Cool!' Natasha with the eye patch says, who you can always rely on to be jealous of everything.

'WHATEVER!'   Clementine tips her head back and chews her pen. 'You're full of baloney, Darcy,' she mumbles under her breath, and just at the moment when I'm about to shout at her I realize that she's right, even if she did use the word 'baloney'. I am talking total rot and Mrs Hay's annoying voice brings the horrid truth to the surface.

'Aren't you moving house this summer, Darcy?'

'Err. Oh yeah,' I say gloomily.

The truth was, I didn't want to move house. I thought I did, but now that moving day is almost here I really actually don't want to do it at all. Why would I want to move house when we have all we need in our already *now* home?

'That's exciting then, isn't it?' she nudges, but I don't feel excited.

'Have you been to see your new house?'

'Yes.'

'I hear it's bigger than where you are now, so you must be looking forward to having all that space?'

No, actually, I am thinking. *No. I am not.* And yes, even though the more newer house looks very nice . . . looks don't really count in comparison to feelings, and right now I'm feeling that it's quite a lot for one human, if you ask me, for their whole world to be upheaved and translated to some new house. All in six weeks. I lean on my hand and stare out of the window. I wonder if I will see the world all very differently once I move house?

I hope not.

'I have a challenge for you all to do over the summer . . .' Mrs Hay says, looking all happy, and that momentarily takes me quite away from feeling worrying.

The room audibly sighs. Groaning.

'We HATE homework!' Matthew moans.

'Miss, don't be tight and make us do bare writing on our break!' Sania adds.

'Yeah, miss, it's meant to be our holiday,' Kemal chips in. 'We've worked so hard all year!'

'Miss, how would *YOU* like it if you had to do work over the holidays?' Thomas gripes.

'This isn't homework . . . and no one said anything about writing. This is a challenge for you – I want you to have a think about something that you want to achieve over the six-week holidays.'

'Guuuuuuuhhhhhhh, miss, that's *dry*.' Mohammed bangs his head onto the desk.

'I've already achieved everything I want.' Clementine shrugs, all smug.

'It's not homework. It doesn't have to be a big challenge but it would be a good idea to set yourself a goal, something you've always wanted to do. Perhaps kick a bad habit like biting your nails or start learning a new language or skill.'

'Sounds like homework to me.' Kemal folds his arms.

'It could be something so small, like maybe

be less grumpy in the mornings. Just try it. It might be nice if when we come back into school we share our progress?'

Everybody moans, but Mrs Hay makes it all better by bringing out a big box of chocolate biscuits for us to share. It's only five minutes before the last bell rings, so we all tuck in. Books flapping and bags smacking and chocolate biscuits flying in the air as we raid the packaging, trying to squish as many cookies into our mouths as quick as possible. They are posh ones that come in a tray. I know it's *all* about taking the ones wrapped up in gold foil. I am not stupid.

And the bell rings . . .

Summer is truly in the air. The sky is a whip of blue and white froth. It's warm, so we wear our pullovers wrapped around our waists. We see the big ones from the oldest year all crying and hugging. They have coloured handwriting all over their shirts from where they've signed them. It's their last day of not being a growed up. *Why are they crying?* I would be

jumping up and down if I didn't have to go to school any more.

'It's all downhill from here,' Will sighs.

'No it's not. I can't wait until I get growed up. You get to have long legs and long hair and eat ice cream in the middle of the night and no one says one thing to you about it.'

'Yeah, but think about all the bills and letters you have to open, all the newspapers with the tiny words you have to learn to read. It's horrible being an adult, everybody looks at you the whole time as if you know what to do next.'

'When you put it like that it does sound exhausting.' I lick chocolate off my thumb, and we wave to some of our classmates as we go out. Some we will see over the holidays. Some we won't. That's how it goes.

'So, are you all packed up?' Will asks.

'We're not moving *just yet*.' I scowl, even though it's not Will's fault. 'My mum keeps telling me I have to pack up my bedroom but I just told her I'd shove all my stuff into bin liners when the day comes.'

'You've got so much junk in there, it's gonna take you ages.'

'Oh, *nag, nag, nag*. Not you too!' I frown and push his arm.

'Sorry, but don't you want your new room to be all . . . you know?'

'I like my room as exactly how it is,' I interrupt.

'You always moan it's small.'

'Well, I've changed my mind. I like small. I like my room how it is. I like things identical to how they are.

I don't really wanna even move.' I see a man washing his car, a ginger tom cat snaking along the wall. 'Anyway, until we *have* to move, I am wanting to have as very much fun as possible!'

'Me too, I can't wait for Spain,' Will says. 'Can't wait to be in the pool with a lovely milkshake.'

'How long are you going for *this* time?' I ask, even though I don't want to hear the horrid answer.

'Five weeks.'

'FIVE weeks? *FIVE* whole entire weeks? Nobody needs to spend five weeks anywhere. It's way too long. You'll get bored.' How DARE he go to Spain for FIVE weeks? WITHOUT ME! How dare he see that gorgeous sunshine without me! He'll no doubt be missing me like madness.

'I won't be bored. I have my cousins and I've got friends there.'

'And what will you do with these cousins of yours?'

'I dunno – probably just what we do every year. Play football, ride our bikes, swim in the pool, sunbathe—'

'All right, are you just trying to deliberately upset me now?'

'You asked!' he yelps. 'You're not seriously annoyed at me, are you?'

'No, I don't care actually what you do, and anyway tomorrow I was only going to invite you to Captain Adventure's Water Park. But I guess I'll just be going alone.'

'Aargh, I love it there.'

'Well, you'll just have to *love it there* in your dreams, I guess.'

Bet that was a right stab to the heart.

'Why do you always have to be so dramatic about everything all the time?'

'Why do you always have to be so annoying the whole time?'

'Listen to yourself – you're the one being annoying.'

OH, SHUSH UP.

We don't hug or anything at the corner. We just say goodbye as usual and then say *See you soon.*

Oh. *Just*. GREAT.

FIVE weeks without Will. FIVE weeks without my only true real actual friend.

Great.

'Will!' I shout as he's walking away. 'Don't die or get eaten by a shark.'

'I'll try not to!' he shouts back.

'Miss you!'

'No you won't!' He laughs and winks at me and I spin around thinking to myself, *I will. I will, like mad.*

*

At home Mum is packing the cookbooks into boxes.

'Hello, monkey, can you pass me the brown tape please?'

'Why are we packing? We aren't going yet, you know.'

'Darcy, we're moving next week! Have you seen how much stuff we have? We are a family of hoarders!'

I throw her the brown tape and stick my finger into the jar of peanut butter.

'Use a spoon please.'

I ignore her. The tape makes a squeaky noise as it comes away from the roll.

'I am so looking forward to having more space,' Mum says. 'I can have all my books on display rather than hidden away in the cupboard. I cannot wait.' She scribbles the words *Cookbooks – Kitchen* on the side of the box in a marker pen and then flumps down. 'How was the last day of school?'

'Fine. We got cookies.'

'Nice. Dad's just picking up Hector and Poppy.'

'We got given homework.'

'To do over the holidays?'

'Yes!'

'What? That's outrageous! What kind of home-work?'

'We got given this diary and we have to write at the start something we are going to try and do over the holidays. Like a challenge. Then we have to fill the diary with our progress, I guess.'

'That doesn't sound like homework to me, D, that sounds like a good idea.' Mum smiles, pushing her hair behind her ear. Lamb-Beth tumbles in from the garden to greet me – she looks all sunny and happy and extra cute. 'What's your challenge going to be then?'

'Maybe, *have fun*?'

'I don't think *have fun* is the right challenge for you. You have the most fun out of anybody I know.'

Technically I'd argue that point and say that Hector has way more fun than me, but anyway.

'I need to think about it.'

'What about to try and keep your room tidy?'

'Err . . . how about not?' I snap.

'How about to not answer back to your mum?'

I would answer but my mouth is clamped together with peanut butter. I open the fridge door with smudgy peanut paws and pour a glass of milk from the fridge, and as I drink it the peanut butter spreads out over my tongue and dissolves.

'So then, are we going to go to Captain Adventure's Water Park tomorrow?'

'Captain what?' *Do* NOT *tell me she's forgotten.*

'Captain Adventure's *Water Park*?' I remind her.

'You know, the one with the doughnut river and the big slide and the wave machine and the hot dogs?'

'Oh no, not that stupid place. No, of course we're not going, Darcy, we've got *so* much to do before we move. We haven't got time to go to a water park.'

'BUT, Mum!'

'*But, Mum* nothing. It's chaos there, Darcy. You nearly drowned about twenty-five times the last time we went.'

'NO, I DID NOT! I am a tremendous swimmer.'

'I didn't say you weren't, but there's so much going on there, it's an absolute nightmare. Plus it's far away.'

'No it's not.' (I think it might be, but still.)

'It is, plus it will be really busy. So, no. Not now we've got too much on.'

'But you promised.'

'When?'

'AGES ago.'

'Yes, probably before I knew we were moving house and your dad was taking on that new job.'

'This is just *typical*.'

'You can't get everything you want, Darcy. Now pop the kettle on please, love.'

GRRRRRRRRRR!!!!!!!! I snatch the kettle off the disc thing it lives on and march over to the sink. I turn the tap on as hard as it will go and water a bit spits down my front but I don't give Mum the satisfaction of looking her way so we can laugh about it. I am cross at her. What a traitor. I AM SO

ANGRY. Great, I get it. So Will gets to go to Spain and I am stuck here in boring same land. I have to just say it . . .

'Before the others get home I just want to say this to you. Loud and clear, I have to get this off my chest and let you know that my feelings are torn apart into pieces. I worked really hard this year at school and was looking so forward to spending the day with you.* I am really hurted right now, because you

* At Captain Adventure's Water Park.

PROMISED. And you shouldn't make a PROMISE
that you can't keep.'

Mum stares at me blankly and says, 'Give it a rest,
Darcy, and stop being so dramatic.'

Chapter Two

WEEK 1/6 OF FREEDOM

Do you think I am in a bad mood or not?

Well, let me tell you something for nothing right this minute. I am in the most *worserest, baddest, horridist* moods of all moods that's *ever even* been dreamed up.

It's because today we are NOT going to Captain Adventure's Water Park, but instead, as a compromise, we are going to the BORING wee-wee baby-child paddling pool. Because it is only 'down the road'. It's my first day of the summer holidays and is meant to consist of uninterrupted FABULOUS mayhem without any annoying stuff, and WHAT ARE WE DOING? We are going to the stupid park with the ugly shallowest puddle of all time inside it.

I HATE the paddling pool because it's an evil unhygienic swamp created for naked snotty babies that take turns, like it's a competition, to wee in it as much as possible, and even though – yes, I admit it – I do wee in the paddling pool myself from time to time, there is a big difference between accidentally swallowing your own wee to swallowing some strange weird two-year-old's wee.

And what makes it even worst?

Donald Pincher is coming.

Mum would say that Donald is a 'friend of the family' but I would say he is a *posh parasite slug that is bratty and snobby and always gets what he wants that we* HAVE *to hang out with because his dad works with my dad.*

HUMPH.

We can see annoying pale smug Donald Pincher already, standing by the ice-cream van with his mum, Marnie Pincher – *shudder.* His pasty body makes him look like an anaemic uncooked croissant stuffed into trunks. And he has bo-moobie woobie wobby boy boobs that are covered in leaky gross melted ice cream from his wilting 99. *Yuck.*

Marnie points and waves enthusiastically. She has on expensive designer sunglasses that I wouldn't mind sitting on if given the chance. *CRACK. GOODBYE,* showy-offy glasses. *Eugh.* We are not on holiday in Portugal, you know. It's not even *that* sunny.

Hector speeds ahead on his scooter. Mum will end

up carrying that *and* him on the way home, no doubt. If I was Mum I would just take that scooter and hurl it over the back of the house so he couldn't bring it anywhere, but Mum says if he doesn't bring it, it will take him ages to get anywhere. So we all have to suffer. It's a domino effect because I'll then have to carry the entire bag of heavy wet towels home. L-O-N-G S-I-G-H.

Poppy is already running after Hector, choosing her ice lolly before she's even reached the van. *Cherry. Strawberry. Bubble Gum. Lemonade. Orange.* I would be running ahead too but Mum's making me carry all this *stuff*. I am panicking, quite badly, about my lolly flavour. I really don't feel that comfortable leaving the responsibility with these beanbag heads to choose me a good flavour.

'The whole gang together!' Marnie screeches and embraces us, bringing us in for a clunky awkward

group huddle. Her shaved armpit is in my face and up close looks like a wrinkly dog's bum. Her elbow clanks into my side – *ouch* – and her purple lipstick leaves a huge sticky smear on my jaw. I know I have to be polite and let the pee-pee wee-wee piddling pool wash it off instead of wiping it off with my fist or Mum will do *that* look like I'm being rude. I'm sorry. It is NOT rude to wipe somebody's yucky mouth juice off your face.

After dumping our stuff down on the 'spot' that Marnie has saved for us (a shady, overcrowded, bird-poo-splattered slab of concrete draped in Marnie's posh towels) we get changed. Annoying Poppy remembered to wear her bikini underneath her sundress but I forgot. Obviously. And she didn't remind me either.

Livid.

Hector and Poppy don't think twice and strip off, then dart into the shallow pool, leaving me all behind as well and everything. Mum goes off to get ice creams with Marnie, even though that means, if my maths serves me right, that technically Donald is getting to be having TWO ice creams because I sawed him having that one earlier! The evidence was all leaking down his chest. I am not STUPID, you know, like all these other immature saddo baby tots, and I can spot a crook a mile off, trust me. Sneakiness behaviour never gets past me!

All these other kids are just running all round the whole place like they never been outdoors before; screaming and squawking as if this cruddy paddling pool is a *great* place to hang. Well, they aren't fooling me.

Poppy beckons me to the water. I have to get into my costume. They don't even have changing rooms in this barren land so it feels like one hundred and a thousand eyes are all staring.

Firstly I wrap one of the towels over my head and body and crouch over, scampering off my shorts. My plan is to quickly wriggle out of them, pop the right leg into the bottom of my swimming costume while dragging the left leg out of the shorts, all in a swift, smooth, sweeping movement like a stunt person. I'll keep my top on, niftily take my arms out of the sleeves, meaning I can haul the top of the cossie and get my arms in the straps underneath the shirt. Finally my grand reveal of my mermaid costume will be on full delightful display.

But instead, once I take a leg out of my shorts, hopping up to put the other leg into the costume, the *idiot* towel slips off me and I lunge forward to reach it, but then I step on a hairy beary solitary thorny acorn that's wearing its stupid spiky conker jacket – *OUCH!* – I jump up, which flings my other leg out of my shorts, springing my costume into the air and into a pile of uneaten sandwiches from somebody else's picnic, and before I know it my bare bum is on view for everybody to see.

As pale as a shelled boiled egg.

'Whoa, careful, Darcy, your full moon is blocking

out the sun!' Donald *chortles* as he arises from the water, lying flat on his belly like some hideous moose beast. His laughter alerts numerous other kids (yes, even ones I never metted) to also laugh *and* point, making me feel like an absolute display cabinet of awfulness. *How dare they laugh though?* They don't even *know* me. I go red and, sound-tracked to the sniggers of strangers, I grab the towel, wrap it round me like a long skirt and, inching in pigeon steps like a *real* mermaid, just not as excellent, reach for my costume, trying to pretend none of this happened. Eyes to the floor, I begin to wriggle the tight costume up my body. It's too small and digging in. I look like I've just eaten fourteen cheeseburgers.

I hate it here.

I step into the lukewarm water. I know that the heating is generated by the vast amounts of hot infant urine dissolved in the water. Wretched. All eyes are watching my toes fiddle in the water, they are wondering why it's taking me so long to get in.

'Darcy! Come on!' Poppy wails.

'I might actually go and help Mum and Marnie with the lollies,' I say, to try and get *out of* getting in.

'No worries, I'll do it!' Donald, the jammy toad, leaps up.

'It's OK, you relax there,' I reassure him. But oh no, up he gets, and it's like watching a blubbery flubbery walrus flop out of the sea. *Great. That was meant to be* MY ESCAPE. And now I'm soaking.

Grrrrrrr! If I wanted a tidal wave to smash me over the head I'd go find one.

I'm wet now. In I go.

There is a snotty child with yellow hair filling up an empty crisp packet with water. Great. Wee and cheese and onion. *Weese and onion*. Hideous. My worserest flavour. I wade in further towards Poppy and Hector. Past the loose rafts made of scraggy, lost plasters, bogey tissues and pigeon feathers. The smears of snot and chewed Ribena straws.

'I'M A SARK!' another boy bellows in my face.

No you are not, I think. I like to play shark. And it's not SARK. It's sHark. *Idiot*.

The middle of the pool is the only decent bit in the whole place. Because it's the deepest bit. But even when you're sitting in the water it only goes up to your tummy button. So boring and babyish. Hector and Poppy are already off chasing each other with makeshift water guns made out of water bottles. Great. I plonk myself there like a hippo and wait for

my fabulous lolly to be hand delivered. I wait. Roll my eyes. Try and warm up. Close my eyes and pretend I am in Hawaii. Accidentally let out a fat wee. Another kid looks at me like, 'Ugh, are you weeing?' and I'm like, 'Mind your own business, you little weirdo, and put a top on.'

Mum's back with the lollies and I completely forget to be waited on because I am a greedy gargantuan moose that's DESPO for my lolly. WAIT FOR ME!

We all rush back to the side. Hang on, why does Donald look so pleased with himself . . . ? Hmm . . . rush, rush, wobble, trip . . .

And then I stub my toe on the step bit to get out. It's all scratchy and cement concrety with bits of pebble and stone. STIIIIIINNNG. *Ooof. Ooof. Hop. Hop. Yawwwwww. Cawwwwwww. Bawwwwwww.* Tears in my eyes. Fizzle. Don't cry. Don't cry. Hold it together. Hold it together. I bite my lip. Squeeze my eyes shut. The pain. *Zap. Zop. Zing. Throb. PANNNG. THIS WOULDN'T HAPPEN IN HAWAII.*

I hobble over to Mum, absolutely freezing, my jaw shaking. This is a nightmare. Hector's lips are already blue. *Chitter chatter.* This isn't a fun day. This is torture. Freezing cold torture.

33

I hate this; forced to spring about in a shallow tepid ditch with loads of unhygienic germified strangers and their yellow wee and jam hands and snot strings and bum juice.

Marnie is very impressed with herself as she unpeels the lolly wrappers with her spiky, purple, painted claws and hands the traffic-light colours out. We could do it ourselves but Marnie enjoys to baby us like that.

'Lemonade for you, Hector. Strawberry for you, Poppy. Cherry brandy for Mollie and me.' She winks at Mum. 'We need all the *brandy* we can get!' she snorts.

Mum doesn't even think it's that funny a joke, I can tell, but laughs back anyway.

'There's a lime for you, Darcy.'

Green? They got me GREEN?

'Green? You got me GREEN?' My face wrinkles up in disgust. It's not that I'm being ungrateful, but WHY would you get me green? Green is one flavour up from basically poo.

Green?

'I thought you liked green?' Mum suggests, licking her delicious cherry brandy icicle.

'Since WHEN have I liked *green*?'

'Well, you didn't mind finishing off all those green sweets in the car.'

'That's different. They were the only ones left – when the green are the only ones available, of *course* you have green, but you don't *choose* green.' I feel dumb, but tears begin to froth in my eyes. It might be from the toe stub. 'Oh, right, I get it, so you lot are just gonna sit there sucking the living daylights out of your red scrummy lollies and I get green.'

'You can have mine?' Poppy suggests, which is kind but her saliva poison is already all over hers.

'Thanks, Poppy, it's OK. I'll have green.'

Mum shakes her head. 'You owe Marnie a thank you, Darcy,' she says sternly. I look at her like my eyeballs have popped out of my head. *OWE? OWE* her a *thank you*?

'Thank you, Marnie,' I say all softy, watching all the smug rat heads around me enjoying their lovely lollipops.

'You're welcome, Darcy, it was Donald that told me you wanted lime.'

Donald said that? That I *wanted* lime?

'Why, what's Donald got then?'

'I think he went for a Nobbly Bobbly.'

Seething.

And before I can even blaze him with my anger, he is off, running towards the arctic puddle, jelly moobies juddering and spilling muffin tops quivering. And it dawns on me that I know I will have to be hanging out nonstop with DONALD this summer. And that I better get used to this wretched boy because he clearly isn't going ANYWHERE!!!!

And I already can't stand the SIGHT of him.
HUMPH!

Slog. Slog. Slog.

Mum and Marnie have boring conversations. I sit next to them for a bit of eavesdropping in case anything funny about Donald arises. Wrapped in a towel, holding my throbbing pink toe, sticky slithers of green lolly juice down my hands looking like alien dribble, and mainly being all depressed, I flop down

on the hard concrete and blow an old crumb towards an ant. The ant is so close he could almost pick up the crumb but he doesn't. He can't turn round and say I didn't *try* to help him.

'Mum. Mum. Mum,' I moan and weep. 'Can we please go home now?'

'You were the one that wanted to come out! You were the one that wanted to go swimming.'

'You can't *swim* here unless you are a rat or a Barbie. I'm bored out of my Brazil nuts.'

'Darcy, how can you be bored? There is *so* much to do. Look, it's a lovely day, the sun is shining-ish, you've got a paddling pool and friends to play with! *Bored!? Unbelievable.*'

Friends? I wouldn't count Donald or my own siblings as my *friends*.

'I don't want to get in the stupid poop-id pool,' I grumble.

'Don't, then,' she snaps.

'Where's that best friend of yours? What's his name – Billy?' Marnie chips in.

'His name is Will.'

'Will, yes, why don't you get him to come down and keep you company?'

'He's in Spain on holiday,' I grumble, feeling so annoyed at him that he's on holiday and I am here doing THIS life.

'Yes, Will and his older sister Annie go away every summer, don't they, D?' Mum tells Marnie while stroking my raggy hair. 'He has family there.'

'Oh, that's nice for him! Lucky for some!' Marnie cackles, rubbing her legs down with some ghastly, gluey-wuey cream.

'So what am I meant to do then?' I humph restlessly. 'I don't have activities with me.'

'No homework you can do?' Marnie suggests. What on earth? She's just as bad as school!

'Well, actually, she does have *one* bit of homework she could be getting on with,' Mum says.

'Ooooh, go on, what is it? I love a bit of homework.'

'Mum?' I ask, to make it very clear that I'm talking to Mum and not Marnie, so butt out.

'She has to set herself a challenge, something to achieve over the school holidays. I suggested tidying her room,' Mum answers, even though it's my business not hers.

'That's not homework!' Marnie slaps her prickly legs. 'Donald gets *so* much homework, but that's probably because he's a child genius and the school want to push him as much as possible.'

Sure. Whatever.

'Why don't you get a job?' Marnie adds. 'That would make a great challenge.'

'A JOB?' Has she LOST the plot. A job? Who does she think I am? A 500-year-old? A JOB?

'Yes, you could try and get yourself a job over the holidays, bit of responsibility never hurt anybody – it would keep you busy, you could learn a new skill and earn yourself some cash too.' She looks at my multi-coloured painted toenails. 'I mean, a creative girl like you – you never know *where* you're going to end up, do you? A job would be great for you.'

MUM! STOP THIS WOMAN AND HER WICKED WAYS!

'I think she's too young for a job, Marnie.'

'Yes, *Marnie*,' I add.

'I had a job when I was your age. I worked as a waitress in my uncle's coffee shop.'

'Darcy's too clumsy to be a waitress.'

'I am not!' And then I immediately remember the many times I've walked into mirrors because I thought they were doors.

'What about babysitting?'

'BABYSITTING?' I gawp.

'That could be a good idea. You love kids.' Mum smiles.

'Yes, but not to be a babysitter,' I argue. 'I'm basically a small baby myself.' I shrink.

'I don't know, I think you would make a fantastic babysitter.' Mum rubs some lip balm on her lips.

'No, Mum. That's a rubbish job. Cleaning up some baby's poo and wee and sick and tears all day. No thanks.'

'All right. We were only trying to help.'

'Wish I had my writing book here.' I rest my head on the fleshy bit of my arm.

'I have some paper,' Marnie says all kindly, but she does have those sunglasses on so I can't be sure if she's not just being a villainous wicked witch. 'Pass me my handbag and let's have a look.'

'There we go,' says Mum. 'That's great. Thank you, Marnie.'

Why can't Marnie just get off her bum and get her handbag herself?

I sling Marnie's posh handbag over to her and she begins to fiddle through it. She pulls out a leather-bound diary, tearing some pages out for me, and then she hands me a pen.

'There we go. What do you say, Darcy?' Mum patro-sizes me down with that voice that swoops high and low like a roller coaster.

'Thank you, Marnie,' I say, which I was going to obviously say anyway.

'Ah, it's nothing, knock yourself out.' She smiles

and then continues talking to Mum about some woman at her yoga class who she hates.

Why don't **YOU** knock **YOURSELF** out?

I nudge over the towel a bit and think about what to write about. I can't get comfy. All the loops of the towel bit are ramming into my pointy elbows and Poppy and Hector keep calling me over to play. But I'm being too stubborn because that pool brings nothing but bad luck and also I hate this swimming costume. It's like Mum forgot I grew or something. I write a couple of words and then scribble them out. Suddenly a toddler in a nappy comes padding over to me. She is soaking wet from the water and has only a few teeth that are spread out like a monster munch crisp.

'What?' I ask her big brown eyes and curly black hair. 'What do you want?' And then she digs her finger up her nose, eyes still fixed on mine. It's hard to concentrate when there is a little baby in a nappy aggressively picking her nose in front of you.

'OK,' I say back, and lean down to the paper again. I don't like it that you can see the dates on the pages. *Mon 24th, Tue 25th, Wed 26th* . . . It's distracting. I like a big clean empty page to write on – *waaaaahhhhhhhhhh* . . . I feel something on my back. 'What is it? What is it?' I ask the baby but she says nothing. Her stubby digit pointing at my back, gargling something jibberish. It all becomes clear.

'That's one of your bogeys, isn't it?' I gag and retch. 'That you just wiped on my back.'

'Ah-hah,' says the baby. Nodding, as though she's *proud*. Like I should be *grateful* for the generosity. 'Hujiwama.' She smiles, pointing at the thing again.

'Hujiwama?'

'Hah.' The baby grins.

'Gross.' I cringe. 'I don't care what you call it, it's disgusting!' I feel so sick about this grey little baby bogey, the lukewarm sluggy goblin that was once lurking in the trenches of rotten disgustingness nostril hole now infesting my back.

BLEUGH. BLEUGH. I roll over like a dog rolling in fox wee at the park, but I probably look more like a pig in mud. *GET IT OFF ME, ATTACK, ATTACK.* I shudder violently.

'What *is* the matter with you?' Mum says, all unsupportive.

'That hideous baby just wiped a bogey on my back. I would be the worstest babysitter in the whole entire world because I hate babies and they hate me. Just in case you still think that would be a brilliant idea.'

'Do you know what would be lovely,' she says in this stern, straight voice, 'would be if you could just come outdoors and *not* be dramatic for once.'

'Hah!' annoying Marnie Pincher chips in. 'Now *there's* a challenge for your school project.'

Oh, shut up, you. It's not a *project*. Like it's something I'm dedicating my existence to. Go away.

'Yes!' Mum laughs. 'That's a great challenge for you, D! But she'll never be able to do it,' she mocks. 'Darcy loves a bit of drama.'

'Yes I will!' I scowl, folding my arms and crossing my brows. 'I can definitely do that, easy peasy lemon squeezy. I bet I can go a LIFETIME without making any drama AT ALL.'

'We'll see about that,' Mum taunts me.

'Oh, yes we will.'

'Darcy, *please* . . .' Marnie twiddles the lolly stick skeleton around in her fingers, chewing on the end. 'You couldn't even do an hour without making a drama out of *something*.'

Oh, how I would love to choke her with that lolly

stick. Annoying wicked witch from nosy land.

'Well then, I bet I CAN at LEAST do the whole entire six-week summer holidays. Without making one bit of drama about ANYTHING!'

And then they both laugh. Right hard. In my face. Giggling. Slapping the ground. *Oo-ha-ha-hardy-ha-ha-heee-oooo-my life-wow-oooo-heee-teee-hoooo-ahhhhhh-hhhaaa-that's funny-haaaa-ha-ha-ha-ha-I can't breathe-I can't breathe-stop it-stop it-too funny.*

And I'm just there. Watching them. Unimpressed.

Thinking, *Just you two* IDIOT *hags wait.*

S-L-O-W B-L-I-N-K.

Donald, the blustering great mammoth, stomps over. 'What's so funny?' he says, drying his nipples off with the towel. *Mubble wubble.*

'Darcy reckons she can do the whole summer holidays without making a drama about anything,' Marnie says, and then Mum begins to laugh again. More laughter. In harmony with the annoying cackles of Marnie and stupid Donald.

And all I want to do is lose my absolute temper and go ballistic and crazy in their faces, but I can't because that counts as drama. I just have to get on with it. Like the dot of an ant that is carrying a bit of pink wafer towards his little hole of a home in the ground. Oh, I get it, so that ungrateful ant didn't want the crumb I blew him earlier but NOW wants this bit of pink wafer. Beggars shouldn't be choosers.

So I fake-smile really hard instead, squinting my eyes really tight shut and say, 'Now if you'll excuse me I have writing to be getting on with.'

DOT AND THE HUJIWAMA

Dot was not a good ant.

He was not quick. Or uniformed. Or tidy. He couldn't march along to the same rhythm as everybody else in the ant army. He wasn't good at passing food down the line in trail training, or helping carry it either. He always lost his balance and ended up dropping the crumb in hand to the ground — which as any ant knows is dangerous because the crumb can fall and injure another neighbouring ant, and/or be picked up by somebody else — a bird, a mouse, a human finger or hoover.

It was a tough job being an ant. It took teamwork, speed, a good eye for treats, and reliability.

Dot was clumsy, wobbly, easily distracted; would talk too much and annoy the other ants,

49

snack as he went and just simply be *not good* at being an ant.

All the other ants had had enough of Dot. And Dot knew it. There was nothing he could do. He would never get a place on the trail and venture outside in the big *bad* world and scoop up fallen treats from the human strangers.

A big day was approaching; the first day of the summer holidays. And that meant there was only one place to go. The Paddling Pool. *Why?* Because it was picnic *galore*. The heat of the summer and the endless free days of no school would mean the concrete (easy speedy, large, scuttling surface, great for following a trail) and grass surrounding would be packed with greedy, carefree children, and *nobody* made crumbs as good as children. They ate like raccoons. Especially toddlers. They dropped food like loose change on a roller coaster. The best kind of food too! Bollards of biscuit crumbs (ideal for carrying; light and robust and stuffed with sugar), kerbs of bread crusts (healthy, full of fibre and carbohydrate which is a *must* for any hardworking ant), rubbles of cheese chunks, puffs of salty cheesy Wotsits (which were brilliant too, so light and airy to carry — some of the stronger ants could carry a whole one themselves back to the colony!). Yes, sponge cake, half-moons of pizza crusts, flecks of dried banana, flakes of coconut, juicy plump raisins, crumbles of pastry and spills and spills of melted shiny rivers of ice cream and sticky lollipop puddles to sail over on a boat made of salted cracker. It was a paradise of fallen heaven. Life was great at the Paddling Pool.

Children were pretty much the scariest thing on earth. When they weren't screaming their heads off or stomping their excitable feet (which meant an awful lot of 'playing dead' for the ants) they wanted to stop and prod or *touch* the ants. Children *love* to follow a slithering ribbon of ants into a sandy hole in the wall.

Other than that . . . there was another very scary thing on earth.

The big Pool itself.

To a child it looks probably nothing more than a shallow oversized puddle. But to an ant it was like the roaring ocean itself. Each splash was a tidal wave ready to drown them in one swoop. They had to be very careful.

It was the start of the new ant year. Summer was arriving and that meant the foraging season. The places on the trail were being appointed by the Queen Ant. This was a very big deal. It was a time for older, more experienced members of the colony to hand over their positions on the trail to younger, faster, fitter ants.

One at a time the ants were called to the Queen's great palace (a human being's baseball cap) which sat, buried, by the roots of the old tree. The Queen wears a cape made from the silver foil of a chocolate bar and looks rather splendid. She only wore the cape at special occasions such as this. Dot was very nervous. He knew he was one of the clumsier members of the colony but surely he'd done enough to prove his weight and worth to the Queen to earn a spot on the trail this year. But he couldn't be certain . . .

'Come in, Dot.' The Queen greeted him warmly from her throne (a ring-pull from a can of fizzy drink). 'Now,' she began, 'I've been thinking long and hard about where to position you, Dot.'

'You have?' Dot was excited, his little ant fingers were crossed, he wanted to be on the trail so badly.

'Yes.' The Queen sighed deeply. 'All the ants love you greatly here, they say how funny and sweet you are.'

'Oh, *stop it*.' Dot blushed, loving the compliments really.

'They say you mean well, that you have a kind nature.'

'I have been known to . . . err . . . have a

soft side.' Dot flexed his little arms – this was looking good, WOW! REALLY? Was he going to be on the trail? HIM? AT LAST! He was ready to kiss the old Queen he was so thrilled! He'd be carrying a ginger-nut biscuit crumb home with the troop in no time.

'Indeed. Which is why I've decided it would be better for everybody if you stayed here, at the colony, and took care of the baby ants.'

'Huh?'

'Don't you agree?'

'The *baby* ants?'

'That's correct.'

'As in the actual babies?'

'Yes please.'

'But–'

'Don't argue with me – you know how much that brings me out in a FURIOUS TEMPER!' the Queen roared. She did have a sassy side and Dot knew it was never a good idea to argue with the Queen. After all, she was the *Queen*.

But the BABY ANTS! REALLY?

Deeeeeeeep, loooooonnnggg sigh.

He was still young, he told himself. There was always time to improve if he trained hard.

But it was later that day when all his ant friends were packing up, leaving the camp for the trail, when Dot really felt the sting.

'Spot?' he asked his best mate. 'Where you off to?'

'Oh, Dot, I've been looking for you all over to share my good news. You'll never guess what . . .

I've been given a place on the trail!' He beamed, elated. 'I'm a *carrier*.'

'Oh. You *are*?' Dot could feel the little blobby tears building up in his eyes. Of course he was happy for Spot, but he couldn't help but feel a pang of jealousy. *How come Spot had been given a place on the trail this time and he hadn't?* And then he saw Speckle – she was moving with the pack also.

'Speckle? You too?'

'Yeah! Great, isn't it?' Speckle was clumsier than *him*, and younger too. 'I'm a spy-er, got good eyes you see . . . I'll be finding those crumbs in no time.' She grinned. 'Well, come on then, Dot, let's go, we've got a picnic to get to!'

'No, no, guys . . . you don't understand . . . I wasn't given a place.' Dot played his sadness down; he didn't want to ruin the big picnic day for his friends.

'What?' Speckle was stunned. 'Wasn't given a place? Why not?'

Dot shook his head.

'So what job have you been given then?' Spot asked.

'I'm . . .' He couldn't lie, not to his best friends. 'I'm the babysitter.'

'Oh. Right,' Speckle said softly, holding Dot's hand in support.

'Chin up, mate.' Spot lightly punched Dot on the shoulder.

And Dot nodded as he watched them fade away to catch up with the senior ants striding ahead valiANTly. He saw some of the other ants laughing at him. A chubby baby ant was slung into his arms. The baby giggled and then sicked up custardy yellowy syrup on his shoulder. 'Oh, cheers, nice to see you too,' he said sarcastically before heading to the nursery, his head hanging low.

The nursery was held inside a human money box. A metal rusty tin tucked away inside the colony. The walls were stuffed with soft findings: the stuffing of teddy bears, tissues, cloth, snags and rags of clothing and sponge. Toys were made of human buttons, flowers, beads. And there were baby ants *everywhere*. Crying, screaming, giggling, rolling, talking, playing, wetting themselves, acting, painting, crawling, *goo-goo, gaa-gaa* mayhem.

Dot still didn't believe this was seriously his job. It wasn't sinking in.

A large ant named Flick welcomed Dot at the keyhole of the money box, which was essentially the staff room. 'Right, Dot, welcome to the nursery. I have a list here of what jobs need doing.' Baby ants already began to crawl up Dot's legs, tumbling around his head like a hat, covering his eyes, dribbling down his cheeks.

'Err . . . OK.' He had never taken care of a baby before in his life.

'If you could just pretty much do everything really.'

'Everything?'

'Yes. I mean, *everything*. If a baby cries it means it wants something. Which happens pretty much constantly.' Dot looked terrified as Flick continued, 'So then you really only have a few options — it means the baby is hungry, thirsty, too hot, too cold, bored, needs a cuddle or needs their nappy changing.'

NAPPY CHANGING?

'Excuse me?'

'OK, fantastic, I'll be in the office nibbling on a grain of rice. I can't wait for the picnic supplies to get back — so bored of rice grains, aren't you?'

'I-I-'

'We're so lucky to have such *brave* and *brilliant* ants to collect food for us. They risk their lives for us lazy losers in here. Still, I'm not complaining!' she shrills. 'OK, good luck

. . . watch out for Tick, she's a biter.' She winked. And as if on cue baby Tick ran over and bit Dot's hand. Hard.

'AARGHHHHHHHH!' Dot screamed.

An hour in and Dot had already been dressed up as a caterpillar, chased the babies, fed them bites of rice grains, mopped up sick, changed a LOT of pooey nappies, wiped tears, painted faces, broke up four squabbles, hugged it out, read a story (which wasn't good enough apparently because they'd heard it before so he had to make one up and *do the voices*). Dot was already exhausted. It was as though time had stood absolutely still. He couldn't stop wondering about the trail. How exciting it must be for Speckle and Spot — they'd be out there, ducking and diving and risking their lives for the colony. As the babies napped, Dot tidied away but he couldn't help but feel sad as he saw the pictures stuck onto the walls of the money box: colourful illustrations done by the baby ants. The drawings were of all the senior, stronger ants of the colony, heroically hunting for snacks.

There weren't *any* drawings of a rubbish babysitter.

But by the end of the day, Dot had made besties with the little baby ants. They loved him. He tickled them and played PEEK-A-BOO with them, he let them sprinkle him with water and tread on his toes, and he'd spin them around until they were sick. He'd sort of had a quite nice day but he was exhausted! In fact, he was pretty sure that this babysitting job was harder than being on the trail itself!

And when Dot's shift at the nursery came to an end, the senior ants returned home to the colony, their bodies bulging with snacks and treats of every type: crisps, wafers, grapes, chips, banana, apple, bagel, chocolate, jellybeans, sandwiches, croissants, shortbread and loads of raisins.

They were high-fiving and smacking wet kisses onto their strong muscles in the colony hall, celebrating their victory. All were alive. And there were lots of goodies to feast on.

Speckle and Spot ran over to Dot, desperate to tell him about their exciting day.

'Gosh, Dot, you won't believe it, there are people like *everywhere* – it's so scary.'

'But so exciting,' Spot added.

'I mean, I've never seen a toe *that* close to, have you, Spot?'

'No, did you know humans have *hairs* on their toes?'

'No,' said Dot. 'No, I didn't know that.'

'How was *your* day?' Speckle asked him gently, remembering to be sensitive.

'Yeah, Dot, how was your day? You look rough.'

'I feel it,' Dot said. 'I feel rough.' And he walked off on his own, back to his walnut shell of a bed, to try and get some rest.

But that night Dot couldn't get any rest at all. He lay awake, tossing and turning. *Why was he so clumsy? Why did he always get things wrong? Why couldn't he be trusted to work on the trail and bring home snacks for the colony?*

And then he had a bright idea.

When the ants of the colony were sleeping soundly, Dot carefully snuck out of bed. He shifted about ever so gently so as not to wake anybody. He was so excited he didn't even notice the red jellybean that Speckle and Spot had left for him as a present outside his shell. Normally he would have loved that; red beans were his favourite.

Scuttle, scuttle, tiptoe, tiptoe, tip . . .

Dot decided that he would make his own trail. With just him. He would do *all* the spying, *all* the carrying, *all* by himself. He would do a hunt. That night. Alone. And this time he would bring back the best, most wonderful collection of treats anybody ever saw. THAT would show them all! THEN they would all see what a brilliant hunter he really was and possibly promote him to senior SENIOR ANT of ALL the trail.

Why didn't anybody ever go out at night anyway . . . ? Surely sneaking out at night meant even more leftover crumbs and NO big ant-stepping human-being feet to watch out for? *Perfect.* This shouldn't take long at all. He was a genius.

Out of the colony and carefully stepping through the passing tunnels towards the little sandy hole, Dot hopped. His tiny heart was thundering nervously in his chest. It was so dark that the exit to the Paddling Pool was almost impossible to see – usually it shone like a little white circle at the top of the tunnel like a miniature moon, but now it was almost impossible to see.

Eventually Dot managed to pop his head out of the hole, into the cool summer's evening. He was right. There were treats everywhere. The ground was peppered with biscuit and crisp crumbs, granules of fallen sugar, bread and cracker crumbs. This was brilliant. He wished he had more arms! But he could do a crumb at a time, keep stocking up, making a big pile. And so he began. He had a simple system going: running into the darkness, collecting a crumb, bringing it back to the pile. Once the pile was high enough, he would then venture from the pile to the tunnel, carrying as much as he could.

Quick. Quick. Quick.

The pile was looking big now! He'd collected *so much* food it was towering. He'd be up all night at this rate, bringing the mountain of food back down. He didn't mind. It was worth it. But he was tired. A full day of babysitting baby ants was draining and he was already falling half asleep.

'Just one more crumb . . .' he sleepily grunted to himself, 'then I'll start packing it down into the tunnel.'

But then a terrible thing happened.

The wind blew.

In one evilly generous breath, a gust of night air swept away Dot's collection. Flecks of his cargo dreamily scattered like a tiny tornado in a snow globe. So this was why they never went out at night! It was too dangerous!

'NO!' Dot screamed, rushing, panicking, desperately trying to scoop up what he could of the crumbs. But then again, the wind blew once more, harder this time, whooshing and pulling and sucking, and poor little Dot was not safe any more. He was trapped. He was drowning in the Paddling Pool!

'Help! Help!' he shouted to the empty darkness. 'Anybody, anything, please!' He sank, little legs scampering, fighting for life. Dot went under. Up again. Another breath. And then down once more. He was so exhausted, he felt faint. Gulping air in the humongous freezing darkness of the pool. He managed to cling onto an empty crisp packet. HUH. UH. HUH. UH. HUH. UH. He breathed heavily — he didn't even have the energy to climb up onto the packet itself. HUH. UH. HUH. UH. ONE. TWO. THREE. LIFT. SLIP. NO! UP AGAIN. UH. HUH. UH. HUH. UH.

Dot, atop the raft of crisp packet — HUH. UH. HUH. UH. HUH. UH — using a floating stick, managed, with his last remaining ounce of strength — HUH. UH. HUH. UH.

HUH. UH — to paddle back to the shore. Panting, he landed on the concrete with a flop. And then he burst into tears. The soaking wet freckle that he was had lost all his crumbs. AND nearly just died. It couldn't be any worse.

'They were right about me,' he sobbed. 'I am useless. I can't do anything right. I only wanted to make them proud of me. I couldn't even do that.' He cried some more in frustration. He'd have to go back home now. Empty-handed. Back to his shell only to wake up tomorrow morning and take care of the babies again.

But that was when he saw it. A gift. From nature.

He wasn't really sure what exactly this gift was. He thought perhaps it was a slug at first, but *this* was different: it was a bit smaller than a slug and not *as* slimy. It was snotty, stringy and wet in places, but also crispy and crunchy and dangly. It was mostly green but white too. It was rubbery and gooey to the touch and could bend.

What was this magical thing?

He sniffed it. Touched it. And then, when he

was brave enough . . . he *licked* it. *Eugh! No.* It didn't taste good . . . but what was it then? What was its purpose?

Another gust of wind rushed past and Dot scooped up the mysterious green thing and quickly scampered down the hole and into the tunnel of the colony.

'It's a Hujiwama,' Dot announced to the Queen the following morning.

'A Hujiwama?'

'Yes, that's right.'

'And what is this . . . Huji-whatsit's purpose exactly?' The Queen inspected it.

'It's . . .'

This was it. His moment to show the Queen that he was a genius. A total, underrated genius.

'A mattress for a bed?'

'Hmmm. Lots of things can be mattresses. Why do we need *this* thing?'

'OK.' Dot looked about for inspiration. 'It's

an umbrella.' He held the green thing over his
head. 'See? Imagine rain coming down.'

'The pistachio-nut shells make excellent
umbrellas.'

'A surfboard?'

'Hmm.' The Queen wasn't convinced. The ants
didn't really *need* surfboards.

'If you bend it . . .' Dot began to bend the
finding so that it curled. 'You've got yourself an
armchair?' He panicked. 'A scarf? A frock?'

'And you say you can't eat it?'

'Well, you can, yes, of course you *can*, you
could, it's just an acquired taste, very . . .
salty.'

The Queen looked at little Dot. Completely
charmed by his enthusiasm but also unimpressed
by his invention. She too was exhausted by his
pathetic, desperate attempts. 'Dot. You are not
to go out at night on your own again, it isn't
safe — you're lucky you didn't drown in the Pool.
All it would have taken was a small gust of

wind and you'd have fallen in.'

Dot looked down at his feet. If only the Queen knew that he had!

'I'm sorry,' he mumbled disappointedly.

'I don't want you to be out there looking for food, that's the trail's job. Your job is to take care of the babies, which is a job that is *just* as important as being on the trail.' She raised her anty eyebrows. 'Now take this Hiji-wiji-scrinchie-whatever-it-is thing out of my palace.'

'Yes, of course, your majesty.' Dot sighed wearily, picked up his Hujiwama and left the baseball-cap palace.

At the nursery Dot lay the big, crispy, sticky,

weird thing down before the big bug-eyed well . . . bugs.

'Good morning, guys.'

'Morning, Dot,' they all sang in harmony.

'Today, I want us to work out what this thing can do.'

72

'Why?'

'Because I said so.'

'But why?'

'Because why not?'

'All right . . . What is it?'

'I don't know. But I've called it a Hujiwama.'

'It's very ugly.'

'It's weird.'

'I licked it.'

All that day Dot and the baby ants tried *everything* that one might do with such a strange object, only to find there were no *real* uses for the Hujiwama at all.

As the ants of the trail returned from yet another successful day of food gathering, back-slapping, joke-sharing and reeling off tips, Dot wanted to roll into a ball and vanish away.

'Sorry we couldn't find a use for your sticky green Hujiwama thing,' one of the little ants said as she waved goodbye.

'Don't worry.' Dot tried a smile. 'Thanks for trying.'

Dot would be a babysitter for ever, confined to the four walls of this silly baby nursery, which was now a *mess* from all the experimentations of finding a purpose for the Hujiwama. Dot was angry, and all of a sudden reached for the big sticky Hujiwama and threw it across the room. 'Stupid thing! GRRRRRRRR!' he roared as it hit the ground with a WHACK.

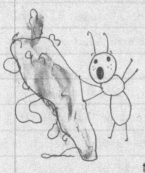

And that was when he saw the most amazing thing. The Hujiwama had lots of bits and things stuck to it.

'Wait a sec . . .' he whispered to himself . . . and then he threw the Hujiwama again.

This time, even more *things* stuck to it. And again. *Incredible.* And again . . . and . . . he couldn't believe it. He'd made an invention.

With his great invention, ants could collect SO much more at a time, on each trip, they could increase their crumb collections by ten – *twenty*, even! They wouldn't have to wait all year round until picnic season because they'd have enough supplies to last all year! Nobody would go hungry ever again!

'Eugh!' Donald interrupted. 'Darcy's picking her nose.'

'Am not!'

'Yes you were, your finger was right up there, dragging down all the goodies.'

'I wasn't. I was imagining how an ant could climb up there and steal a bogey out of your nose.'

'Weird. Why would you want to be doing that?'

'We don't all eat our bogeys, Donald.'

'Be careful, Darcy – seems to me that somebody's getting a little bit too *over-dramatic* . . .'

But nobody was going to listen to Dot. Or his ideas about the Hujiwama. Even if it was a revolutionary invention. The Queen had no patience left for him, and most of the senior ants didn't even know who he was . . . only that he took care of their . . . precious babies . . . unless . . . wait . . . that was it. Dot had an idea.

'I like it,' Flick from the nursery spat between chews of cake crumbs. 'A show! It's great. Something for the parents.'

'Yes!' Dot nodded enthusiastically. 'We have so many talented ant-lings in class and I think it would be nice as a way to say thank you to our senior ants to put on a show for them.'

'Good idea, Dot. I'll tell the Queen.'

Dot clicked his heels together, scampering back to the nursery. He had lots of work to do.

Inside the auditorium of an empty pizza box that evening, thousands of ants gathered to watch the baby ant show. Even the Queen was

present, sitting in her royal bottle-top box, with her silver-foil cape across her shoulders. She winked at Dot as if to say, 'I always knew this was the job for you.'

The lights went down and the curtain (a label of a T-shirt) went up.

Baby ants dressed as the senior ants stomped on stage. The parents laughed their heads off – they loved seeing their little ones pretending to be big and strong. The little ants flexed their muscles and puffed out their chests just like the trail members did, growling and wiping sweat off their heads. It was going well.

'All day we work hard!' one of the baby ants grunted in a big deep voice, imitating her dad.

'Yes, I'm so tired,' another added.

The audience laughed.

'Me too.'

And then down came crashing a bunch of baby ants dressed as a human foot. Their little faces were painted orange and glittery like toe polish. The ants in the audience clapped and laughed their heads off as baby ants screamed and ran in fear from the foot. WAAAAHHHH! The human foot continued to stomp.

'Ahhhhh! Run for your lives!' a baby ant said (who wasn't the greatest of actors).

'No, be still, play dead, don't move!'

'Oh no! Where's that great excellent crumb I just found? It was birthday cake!'

'Nooooo!'

'If only we had more hands, more time and fewer obstacles in our way.'

And then on stage came the tiniest of all the baby ants, and the audience cooed at his cuteness. He was short and fat and dressed like the green, sticky thing that Dot had found and he was holding it, proudly, in his arms.

'But wait, guys, don't panic! Have you seen this great thing?'

'Huh? What is that?'

'*This* is a Hujiwama.'

The Queen did not seem happy. She growled and gave Dot, who was watching nervously from side of stage, the evil eye. *Why was this delusional ant still going on about this stupid Hujiwama thing?*

'Oh, wow!' said the baby ants dressed as the big ants. 'What does it do?'

'Look, you've been wasting so much time, risking your life for a single crumb. Watch what the Hujiwama can do.' And the green thing was thrown across the stage and, as planned, collected up with it hundreds of crumbs. And again, and again.

The audience began to whisper and murmur

amongst each other. They began to see
what the play was saying and they were
impressed.

'Oh my goodness, look how many crumbs are
stuck to that now! That will feed the colony
for weeks!'

'But there is one problem.' Another baby ant
took off her senior ant costume. This was the
serious part of the show, the moral message.
'We don't know where to get any more of
these Hujiwamas from.' The tone of the show
changed. 'Although they are an incredible
invention, this is the only one we've found.
But please, if you—'

'There are hundreds of them!' shouted Dot's
friend Spot from the audience. 'Out there, up
there by the Paddling Pool! Loads of them,
everywhere!'

'Yeah!' Speckle joined in. 'Humans pick them
out of their noses, roll them into little balls and
throw them on the ground.'

Dot couldn't believe what he was hearing and neither could the Queen as other ants began to join in.

'There's an endless supply of them!'

'Sometimes they wipe them on the wall when nobody's looking.'

'Sometimes they *eat* them.'

'Eugh!'

Dot couldn't help but step onto the stage. 'They do?'

'Yes. They're everywhere. Humans call them *bogeys*!'

Dot felt like his magic had been ruined a bit now that he was learning the truth about the Hujiwama. He thought he had found an excellent invention that nobody had ever heard of, but all the ants had seen these green things before.

The Queen stood up from her royal box. *Uh-oh. This wasn't looking good.*

But she clapped. Other ants joined in. And clapped too. A standing ovation!

'Dot, you have been a true credit to yourself,' said the Queen proudly. 'Your invention is a marvellous one that shall be added to the training of the trail. I think it will be time-saving, energy-saving and a little bit of fun too! Well done!' She beamed. 'And well done to the baby ants too, for their brilliant show and reminding us that fun is meant to be had at all times.'

Dot blushed with pride. He and the baby ants bowed and hugged and bowed again and blew air kisses. And the ants all clapped and immediately ran up the tunnel to the Paddling Pool, where they all went hunting, not for crumbs this time, but for the very best bogeys they could find.

But not Dot. He was quite happy in the nursery, playing with glitter and glue with the babies in the nursery, where he belonged.

I finish writing. Next time I see an ant I'll think of Dot. And Spot and Speckle. And next time a baby wipes a bogey on my back – IF there is a next time – I'll think of a Hujiwama.

My elbows have all sore red marks in them from where I've been leaning. *Ouch.* I do feel calmer and happier though. Writing is like that. It mellows you down, cos writing lives somewhere in between daydreaming and wishful thinking.

I hear him before I see him. Stomping over. His scream. His crying. His moaning scrunched-up face. It's Hector. *Apparently* Poppy won't let him join in with the game that her and her brand-new best friend (that she only met like four seconds ago which she **ALWAYS** does every time we go **ANYWHERE**) made up. He is dripping wet. And freezing cold.

'All right, all right.' Mum calms him down. 'You're just tired and hungry.' She picks up a towel, scoops him up in it and folds him onto her lap like a small prawn. 'There we go.' She kisses his head. 'Let's make a move. Darcy, go and get Poppy, it's time to go home. Get your things together.'

And that is when I notice that my story has blown away with the breeze, just like Dot, face down in the water of the paddling pool. Ink washed off, the pages weeping.

My story is drenched. Completely ruined.

WAAHHHHHHHH! I spent absolutely ages on that! I want to shout at Hector for crying and being a baby winge-head, and at Poppy for leaving Hector out in the firstest place and making him cry.

But just when I'm about to yell my head off

I spy all eyes on me. Waiting for me to lose my temper. I just have to calmly begin getting dressed as though nothing ever happened, to look as *undramatic* as humanly possible.

'Never mind.' I shrug.

Chapter Three

DARCY BURDOCK'S SIX-WEEK CHALLENGE: TO NOT BE SO DRAMATIC

It even LOOKS ridiculous. Dad reads it and chuckles over my shoulder. 'Brilliant,' he snorts. 'Absolutely brilliant.' He tuts his head as he picks up his sandwiches and heads out the door for work.

HA-HA. NOT FUNNY.

My stupid ant story is drying on the stupid washing line with clothes pegs holding it up. I absolutely hate myself for putting myself in this undramatic padlock challenge.

It is a brand-new spanking day and this day is a

house day, I think. Mum keeps telling us to go and play in the sunshine because it's a 'lovely day', but that means GET OUT OF MY HAIR SO I CAN PACK THE BOXES UP.

Poppy's friend Timothy has come over to play. He has bought a bag of yummy chocolate-covered animal-shaped biscuits with him and a collection of elastic bands. 'I collect them,' he says about the bands.

'OK. Cool.' I shrug.

Lamb-Beth is springing about like she's all new borned, munching on the grass and lazing in the sunshine. SHE'S SO CUTE I COULD EAT HER UP (but in a vegetarian way). Hector is driving his toy cars up and down her back.

'What do you want to do then?' Poppy asks us both, hands on hips.

'Collect some more elastic bands.' Timothy begins running around the garden, as if there will be elastic bands

growing like flowers. What's wrong with him? Why's he so obsessed?

'Why don't we pling them over the garden fence?' Poppy suggests. 'Could be fun?'

'No, because then we will lose them.'

'We can just go and knock on their door if we lose them.'

'What if they're not in?'

'They probably might even be in, actually,' Poppy argues. 'Look at my mum, she's *always* in.'

We all look at Mum trying to pack up boxes all by her owned self. I feel a bit bad on Mum because she's sort of become that parent that other parents just *dump* their kids on because she's always in and Dad works long hours. It's because Mum is a self-employed art person that people think is just always hanging *around*.

'Mum is so lucky. She gets to never be by herself.' Poppy is thrilled with her sentence. Mum overhears and rolls her eyes. I don't think she is *quite* as lucky as we think.

'There's a funfair near where my mum works,' says Timothy. 'It has a big wheel and a roller coaster and even a ghost train.'

'Cool,' Poppy says. 'I love the funfair.'

'I wish we could go to the fair now,' Timothy says wistfully, 'but my cousin got trapped on a roller coaster upside down for fifteen weeks. All his hair and body grew the other way. That's why he's so tall like a giant and has an afro up to HERE!' Timothy points to the sky.

'Yeah, well one time I went to the fair and I went on this big such scary ride that said you had to be twelve and as tall as a dad to go on it, and guess what?' Poppy leaves Timothy in suspense for a few seconds. 'I. Went. On. It.'

'You said that at the start,' I mumble.

'*And*' – I can tell Poppy is about to lie because she is panicking that her story wasn't interesting enough – 'I nearly fell out and my shoes fell off and they landed on an old dog's head.' She doesn't make eye contact at this point. 'No, no, actually, they landed on his ears, one shoe on one dog ear and one another shoe on the other ear.'

I don't bait Poppy up. But I don't agree with her either. I just let her lie sit there. Like an awkward chair stuck to the ground that nobody can get round. Then I think of something. 'Hey, why don't we *make* a funfair?'

'How?'

'We can make one in the garden – look, using this swing, this can be a . . . look, if we tie this to here and wrap that around that . . . Poppy, go and get the big beanbag.'

'OK, OK.' Poppy darts off into the house.

'What are you doing?' I hear Mum ask from indoors, but Poppy knows that it's probably best to ignore that probing nosy question. So I don't go in the house to avoid confrontation.

'Darcy!' Timothy says. 'This can be another ride. Jump from stone to stone without holding onto anything.'

'Yes, that's good. I'll get some pens and paper and

make signs. We need prices too. I'll get some buttons to be the tokens to get on the ride.'

'What about this too?' Timothy is so excited his eyes are going to bulge out of his head.

'You dangle like a monkey over the washing line . . . no . . . no . . . like a zip wire, oh my days! Like a zip wire!' He giggles uncontrollably, his voice goes all squeezy. 'I've always wanted to go on one. What we need is a tyre or a coat hanger.'

'OK! Yes!' I begin to rummage about for the necessary equipment. 'Good idea, Timothy.'

'I'm back, look!' Poppy squeals. 'I got the big beanbag and all these other cushions too. I found a rubber duck. I thought that could be in the fair too.'

'Yes, like those things you catch on hooks! We need prizes.'

'And candyfloss!'

'And Lamb-Beth can be a ride aswil!' Hector

excitedly suggests sitting on my lamb's back, but I shout at him NO so he changes his mind, thank goodness.

'If only we were at my other cousins', they have a basketball hoop in their garden.' Thanks, Timothy, for that POINTLESS unhelpful comment.

'But what about this? This can be a basketball hoop.' Poppy, not wanting to let Timothy down and wanting our house to be just as appealing as his cousins', just picks up a flowerpot, tips it upside down, shaking the soil *and* plant out. It thuds to the ground.

Poppy realizes immediately that it's naughty but she was overexcited and quickly just scoops and scrambles up the dirt and plant and places it nicely in the corner. 'Here, if we leave this here in the tree it can be a basketball hoop. And here's a ball.'

'Wait. Who is that?' Who do I see with my own eyes trampling through the house making his way into the garden?

DONALD PINCHER!

Oh, what's *he* doing here? Just coming to completely ruin everything ever. WHO invited him? MUM, I'm betting.

'Hi, guys!'

'Hi, Donald.'

'Look how cool this is.' He swipes a plastic grey thing in the air. 'It's a sword. And look here' – he whips out more grey plastic from behind his back – 'a shield. And look at these . . .' He reveals some packets out of both pockets. 'Stickers.'

'Cool!' Hector claps. 'What stickers are they?'

'Stickers *not* for sticking.'

'He only asked,' I bite back. 'Why are you here anyway? Your mum doesn't work.'

'My mum's going furniture shopping or something.'

'Why didn't you go with her? I love furniture shopping.'

'Because once I pooed in the fake model toilet at the house shop.'

'Oh no! That's a bad mistake!' Poppy laughed.

'It was *no* mistake.'

'Oh.'

'So I'm not allowed to go with her, *but* to sweeten the deal Mum got me this sick sword and this shield and these stickers. And guess what also . . . ?' He lets the question hang but looks so smug so I can tell it's gonna be something amazing. 'I might need braces too.'

'Braces?' That's it. I am DEAD with jealousy.

'Yeah, Mum says right now I'm pretty much a handsome nine-out-of-ten stud but I need to get the braces to make me a ten-out-of-ten stud.' Donald then begins thundering around the garden, flashing his *sword* about in his imaginary universe that nobody else is invited to.

'Metal all on your teeth for ever?' Poppy asks innocently.

'Maybe so. Cool though, huh?' Donald swaggers about. 'All the rappers have them.'

I think Donald is ridiculous.

'So what are you goats doing then? What's all this stuff?'

'We're making a funfair.'

'Kinda cool. OK.'

'What's that?'

'A plant pot slash basketball hoop, isn't it obvious?'

'Decent. Gimme a ball then.'

Donald lifts the football up in the air and lobs it at the plant pot. It skittles nicely into the pot. 'Sweet!' And then the pot falls off the tree, topples to the ground and smashes into pieces.

'Donald!' I scream.

'Bad luck,' Donald chugs, as if it's somehow MY bad luck that HE broke the thing. GGRRRRRR.

HEART BEATING. Stay calm. Stay calm. I wrap my fists into balls. I can't make a fuss because I promised, *promised* I wouldn't be dramatic. AND I don't want to draw attention to the fact that we've broken a plant pot or Mum will get stressed and cancel our fun game. Poppy looks to me to see if I'm about to blow up but I keep my cool, chill, cold. 'Don't worry, it's just some pot,' I say. 'No need to bother Mum with it.' Poppy looks relieved.

'We can try and maybe play this game too,' Timothy says. 'Finding the elastic bands.' *What* is it *with Timothy and these stupid elastic bands?*

'There's no elastic bands here, Timothy,' Donald sneers, 'although we can try playing *this* game.' He picks up an elastic band and pings it at me.

'Oi!' Timothy shrieks.

'Ouch!' I squeal. 'Donald, don't, they are Timothy's elastic bands. He collects them.'

'What *for*? Who even needs this many elastic bands?'

'NONE of your business. IF Timothy wants to collect elastic bands, well then, he just CAN and it has nothing to do with YOU!' I a bit shout.

'I'll just do it again. Look. See?' Donald then takes another one of Timothy's precious bands and flicks it at me again. It hits my cheek.

'Donald, *stop* it NOW!'

'You're just a scaredy cat. It's such a boring game anyway. *Find the elastic bands*, please. It's like something my grandad would have played when he was like five.'

'I like it,' Timothy mumbles.

'Yeah,' Poppy adds. 'None of us ask you why you got that sword for.'

'Poppy, the sword speaks for itself.'

'It says . . . MY NAME IS DONALD AND *I* AM SO ANNOYING.'

'Errr. No it does not, Darcy. Nice try.'

'Try out one of rides – here, sit here, Donald.' Poppy ushers him to the swing, patting the seat.

'What does it do?'

'You have to sit down first. Here, give me your sword and your shield.'

'No way, only a fool lowers their weapon,' Donald says in his stupid lispy voice, knowing all words like *weapons* at the tip of their tongues.

'Sit then.'

Donald sits on the swing. We hadn't exactly talked through how the ride was going to work but I was quite happy watching Poppy improvise the components of the ride on the spot but then Donald takes over, like he does with EVERYTHING.

'I know,' he interrupts. 'I'll hug my arms close to

my chest, like a vampire.'

'Yes, cross them over your heart.'

'That's how extreme sport types do free-falling activities,' Donald informs us. 'I mean, if you want your funfair to be half decent you have to know these types of things.' He drops his sword and shield in his excitement and rocks his body backwards and forwards, his fat tummy poking out of his shirt. 'And what do you have in terms of seat belts?'

'Err . . .'

'Timothy, would you please mind passing me the skipping rope?'

Timothy comes close with it. 'You're not going to strangle me, are you?'

Donald snorts. 'Pass it here.' He begins wrapping the rope around his bulk. 'This will make for a much more convincing real ride.' Donald, as if he's a rock climber preparing to abseil down a cliff face, checks the sturdiness of the rope. It *is* looking morer like a real ride.

'OK, now, Poppy, perhaps wrap me up a bit tighter?'

'With pleasure.'

Poppy, with the skipping rope, wraps Donald up so much like a cowboy would a villain with a lasso. He is completely tight like a worm in bandages.

'I can't move,' he wimps.

'Good. That's like a real ride.'

'Yes, good work!' Donald praises.

Poppy moves the beanbag and the other cushions to the other end of the garden.

'Get those swimming goggles!' Donald cries.

'What for?'

'Stop asking questions! Just wrap them over my eyes!'

Poppy, snorting with laughter, does as Donald says and wraps the goggles over his eyes.

'You don't have to be so rough! The rubber is pulling on my eyebrow hairs – ouch, watch it!'

'I'm trying! If you weren't so sweaty it wouldn't be so hard.'

'That's my skin you've got there – aargh, Poppy, can't you be a bit more gentle— Ow-ow.'

'OK, they're on. Great! Let the ride begin!'

'What about this?' Poppy then offers him the rubber duck.

'No, we have no purpose for that in th—'

And Poppy shoves the duck in Donald's mouth.

Timothy, Hector and I are crying our eyes out with laughter. Tears are streaming down our cheeks watching Donald wrapped up as a worm with swimming goggles and a plastic duck shoved in his mouth swinging on the swing. Donald begins to laugh furiously too now at the whole thing. Poppy can barely begin the ride we are all laughing so much.

'DOH LIT LEN!' he mouths in nonsense.

'I think he means *do it then*, Pops!' I say, and so Poppy begins to push. Donald is quite a heifer so Timothy and I join in, pushing and swinging and pushing and swinging and pushing and swinging and pushing and swinging, and Donald is *WEEEEEEEEEEEEEEEIIIIINNNNNNGGGGGGGG* AND *WOOOOOOOO-HOOOOOOOOOIIINNNGGG* AND *AHHHHHHHHHHH-HHHHHAAAAAAA-IIIIINNNGGG!* And the swing is lifting and throwing so much with the momentum of the *backwardsing forwardsing* that the back legs of the metal frame are tipping and lifting out of the ground, springing up and down. Then, suddenly, Timothy just begins to freely ping elastic bands at Donald, catapulting them so hard it's like he just wants this one free moment to get his own back on Donald for being totally vile about his bands. And Poppy spontaneously reaches for the hose and squeaks the tap on. Lamb-Beth ducks for cover as Poppy gushes water at

Donald too. Spraying a fountain of water all over him.

'WAAAAAHAHHH!' Donald snorts. 'It's frebbing cold!' We are laughing even harder now as Donald, all of a sudden, flings into the air, higher than any of us could've possibly even ever dreamed of, like a chubby rocket, like a rugby ball – it's absolutely wonderful. The yellow duck flies out of Donald's mouth and Donald is soaking wet and screaming, 'Look, guys! Look at me! I'm a superhero!'

And just at that moment, Mum steps out into the garden.

No, MUM, GET BACK IN, GET BACK IN, NOT NOW, NOT NOW, and it's like time stops. Like it's actually frozen at the funfair, and then Marnie steps out too. *NO! WHY AREN'T YOU AT THE BORING FURNITURE SHOP, MARNIE? WHY ARE YOU BACK SO SOON? WHY DID YOU HAVE TO SEE DONALD LIKE THIS?*

And eventually Donald falls to the ground, immediately completely missing the cushioning of the beanbag and smacks onto the hard cold concrete floor with a walloping whack.

OH NO.

It all seems to happen so slowly. The crumpling frowns of Mum and Marnie, sewing their faces together in anger, Poppy, Timothy, Hector and I – gawping. Lamb-Beth stunned. And then, that little weasel brute piece of crud, looks up to his mum and cries, 'They made me do it! They were playing dungeons and they strapped these goggles to my eyes and tied me up with this skipping rope and rammed a stupid yellow duck in my mouth.'

HUH?

He adds, 'They were being so crazy, they even smashed a plant pot at the wall for no reason.'

WHAT?

I cannot believe what I am HEARING. I am so livid and raging and crazy and about to explode absolutely everywhere like some diseased monster. I am TREMBLING. But I have to keep calm, I'm not going to give that blasted beast of a boy the pleasure of seeing me flop at my challenge too.

'LIAR!' Poppy shouts. 'You are a liar!' *Awwwright, Poppy!* 'We wasn't playing dungeons – we were playing funfair. And at the fair you play *fair*! YOU wanted to go on that ride and you were having FUN at the FAIR, FUN, FAIR!'

Nice one, Poppy!

'*And* YOU broke the plant pot.'

Marnie and Mum don't know who to believe as they cross their arms and be all so very cross with us. I am keeping my cool. I can't believe it. I AM SO IMPRESSED WITH MY OWN SELF RIGHT NOW. WHAT IS GOING ON?

'Darcy, you should've known better, you're the big sister. What if Hector had hurt himself?' Mum spits all cross.

'Yes, but Hector didn't go on a ride though, did he?'

'Stop answering me back, madam. That's not the point. Imagine if he stepped on some of the broken pot or Donald fell on top of him?' OK, *she does have a point there.* 'It was irresponsible of you.

We are meant to be packing up to move, but I let you have your friends over and play in the sunshine and this is the reward I get?'

Donald cries, 'My arm, my arm.' Fat blubbery, chubbery tears are squeezing out of his porky little  eyes and Mum looks at me and shakes her head.

'You should know better, Darcy.'

I AM SO READY TO VOMIT UP MY A N G R O S A U R U S ALTER-EGO absolutely EVERYWHERE. I can't even stand to look ugly pugly hideous Donald in the face for one more second. Am a bottle of fizzy drink ready to explode.

'I just—' I begin.

'Just go up to your room – go on, get out of my sight,' Mum says, and I know better than to argue.

ANGROSAURUS REX

RUUUUUUUUUUUUOOOOOOOOOOOOORRRRRRR!
ROOOOOOOOOOOOOOOAAAAAARRRRR!

   THE ANGROSAURUS REX was banished
from the town. She lies in a desolate, derelict
cave all by her actual OWN self, having to
eat dry boring bits like old bugs and leaves.
There are NO shops near her and that makes
her MADDER because her most best foods
are chips with salt and vinegar drenched on
them and thousands of MALTESERS. She
cannot feed the starved monster inside her, and
although her belly groans she has to live like
this, in these hideous circumstances, and perhaps
even BE FORCED to maybe even MOVE house

soon too — can I just add — cradling her
hungry belly, howling at the mad red moon
until a chance comes when she can get back to
normal and be angry once more. Only five more
weeks to go of these STUPID, WRETCHED
summer holidays and she can return once more.
But until then . . . her VICIOUS ANGER
MUST BE STORED DOWN . . .

MMMMMMMMUUUUUUUUUUUUUUUH
HHHHHHWWWWWWWWWWWAAAAAA
AAAAAAAI

I HAAAAAAAAAATTTTTTEEEEEEE
YOOOOOUUUUUU, DONALD PINCHER!

I HATTTTTTTTTTTTTTTTEEEEEEEE
YOOOOOUUUUU.

I HATE YOUR FACE.

I HATE YOUR HANDS. AND NOSE.
AND HAIR. AND LEGS. AND FEET.
AND TOES. AND BODY. AND VOICE.
AND IDEAS. AND SUGGESTIONS. AND
LISPY LIES. AND YOUR STICKERS

THAT AREN'T MADE FOR STICKING.
   WHAT ARE THEY EVEN FOR THEN IF
THEY AREN'T MADE FOR STICKING?
   GRRRRRRRRRRRRRRRRRRRRRRRRRR

Knock knock . . .

It's Mum.

'You OK, bug?'

'Uh-huh. Come in.'

'What you doing?'

'Nothing.'

'Donald has to go to the hospital. They want to check him over. He has two black eyes.' Mum tries not to laugh at me trying not to laugh. 'Don't you dare . . .' she warns.

'I wasn't.'

Chapter Four

WEEK 2/6

'I KNEW this idea wouldn't work!' Dad grumbles at me. 'You said you'd have *no problem at all* piling all your belongings into bin bags!'

'And that's exactly what I've done!' I argue back. The problem is, they've all mostly split. Big black sacks with wormy octopus-like tentacles of colour splurging out of every crack.

'Not like this. Not the night before we MOVE!' He is really angry. 'WHAT even is all this stuff?'

'It's my precious things!'

'This Robin Hood outfit that you wore to a fancy-dress party when you were seven is not a *precious thing*.'

'Well, maybe I might need to go to a Robin Hood party in the future one day.'

'You won't fit in this!'

'Maybe I like the memory.'

'BIN IT!'

'All right. Calm down, Dad!' And they have the nerve to call ME the dramatic one, PLEASE!

'I don't know why you have all these clothes that you never wear. I can't remember the last time I saw you in this dress, or these striped leggings or that Santa hat, or this wig.' He rifles his hands through all my books and old toys and papers and games and blankets and scrap books.

'My new room is much more bigger – you said I will have much more space!'

'Yes, for actual stuff, not for *rubbish*. When was the last time you used this tangled-up slinky?' He throws it at the wall where it slides to the floor and wriggles like a multi-coloured ferret. 'Part of moving house is to begin again.'

'I don't want to *begin again*.' I can't help it. I turn away into my wardrobe and cry, gently, softly, not dramatic, and all my multi-coloured clothes are the only ones that see me do it. I mustn't be dramatic. I have to hold it together. I squeeze my eyes shut and pretend I am in an action film at the breaking point when they are about to die. I whisper, all breathy as if the main camera is zooming in close on me, *I have to hold it together. For myself. For my family. For Mrs Hay and my form teacher Mr Yates.*

'You know the van's coming first thing. I just don't get why all you've packed is nonsense and none of your actual stuff. I mean, look at th—'

BANG. Dad bangs his head on my shelf.

'OW!' he roars, immediately taking on the character of a scary bear. He knocks a puzzle of 'the great big jungle' off the shelf and all the pieces drop to the floor and jumble up. Dad says some bad words.

'Ooh, I've been looking for that pu—' I begin, but Dad is NOT impressed. He rubs his head. He is bright red and livid.

'I can't do this right now.' Dad shakes his head. 'I'm going to finish making dinner.'

And he walks out. Leaving me like a sad old person that owns a jumble-sale junk shop that nobody wants to come to.

WHAT AM I GOING TO DO? THERE IS STUFF EVERYWHERE. Piles of books, stacks of writing pads, biro-drewed-on Barbies, creased maps and posters where the folds are worn cracks. Tennis rackets, ice skates, roller blades, badge-making kits, paints, sketch books, a guitar, a recorder, a violin that I've never even touched. A hula hoop. And it occurs to me. All this stuff that surrounds me are the things I've said I'd do that I've never done. I've never stuck at anything. Ever.

And I just have to put the radio on, keep my head down and start packing only what I really need to take with me to the new most ugly wretched scary house. And YES, it is scary. Scary, because it's even more big. And it's not ours. And I don't know it. So it's strange. It's the unknown. It's a bit much to ask us to move into somewhere that I've never stayed the night in. I haven't even had a chance to check out their ghosts or whatever. This makes me cry harder. Then I rub my feet on the wall and calm down.

Knock knock . . .

'Little pig, little pig, let me in.'

'Not by the huge yellow spots on my chin,' I mumble, wiping my tears away.

It's Poppy. She twists the doorknob and lets herself in. 'How's the packing going?' she asks me, and she sits on the bed with amazing gorgeous Lamb-Beth all snoozing on her lap.

I want to say IT'S THE WORST THING IN THE WORLD, but I'm being very good at not dramatizing anything so I just say, 'It's all right. How about you?'

She looks taken aback, to be frank. 'Oh, easy peasy, I did it ages ago.'

We all know MUM did it for her. But whatever.

'Dad told me to tell you that the jacket potatoes are soonly ready.'

''K. Coming.'

If you tasted Dad's jacket potatoes you would find it hard to believe that he was in a bad mood. They are

perfect. Cracky salty skin and fluffy white buttery indoors. Cheese, hot beans, more cheese. Melty, melty comfort. Dad did a very good extra-nice treat and put a spoonful of tuna mayonnaise on the side of the plate. He winks at me. THAT means we are friends again.

BUT . . .

AARGGGGGGGGHHHHHHHHHHH! THE ROOF OF MY MOUTH. SO BURNT. SO. SO. SO. SO BURNT. PEELS! AGH! IT

STINGS AND RINGS AND
MONSTER STRINGS OF
FLESHY TOP OF MOUTH
ARE HANGING DANGLING
ALL DOWN. OUCH!

Toss, toss, hot potato on my
tongue, mouth like a chimney for
the hot air to *hoot toot* out of. Steamy, steamy. Act
normal BUT don't spit it out like you usually would.
Hide the heat. Through watery eyes I force the hot
mouthful of potato down. My nostrils flare as it slides
down my neck. Burning. Raw. Ripping.

'You all right, Darcy?' Mum asks me.

'Yip,' I croak very *undramatically*, I truly
must say. When I want to bawl my eyes
out. And I hop upstairs to continue
sellotaping my amazing life into a
box.

After finally my whole entire
world is boxed away, I lie
flip flop into my bed.

My head is spinning. Imagining all my precious belongings and possessions all stacked up, all silently budged on top of one another in silence. My little quiet items, all thinking I've left them behind. What about all the things that I've thrown away. Cold leftovers with the rain pinging off them.

I can't stop imagining my heart out about who will live here after us. What will their lives be like? What kind of people are they? Will they be happy here?

And then I start to feel so sad to have to say goodbye to this great old house thing that's kept me happy and safe for all these years. Even when I've punched the walls of it and rolled down the stairs of it in a sleeping bag and scribbled bad words on the skirting board, all it's ever done is be a most loyal friend to me. All it's ever done is looked after me and my family.

I begin to write . . .

GOODBYE, HOUSE

It's goodbye to the house where I grew up
where my dreams sat bottled on table tops
where the walls listen in on my ideas
and the heat of bed sheets soak away tears
where the old staircase always knows your name
and the pumping pipes play up like a game
dust hangs in crowds of fingertip touch clouds
rust clangs round where our memories are found
the sun stains, the bleach spots where my things
sit are weird shapes of absence since we have
left the screw that was loose, the garden a mess
creaks on the boards, I will never forget

the same blooms in spring, the way the light came

laughter paints the walls of the rooms we're in

marks on the doorframe of our growing heights

the fights, the tickles, magic cosy nights

we cry, we toddle, we play, jump and dance

inside four walls that make a *building* ours

we drew on your walls, we flooded your floors

we made cracks from the bangs of slamming doors

we got locked out, Dad would climb in the drain

tidy you up then mess you up again

thanks for snuggling me down, keeping us safe

we made our own paradise in this place

your comforting touch, nothing could replace

the trust of your clutch that I met each day

a family lived here before we did

that loved you and knew you just like we did

new people will love you just like we do

and their stories will become yours soon too

keep them happy, keep them warm, give them love

pass onto them all the smiles you gave us

and even though we are moving on now

you will always be my best ever house
we burned bright in you, now we turn off lights
hard to say *goodbye house*, without saying
goodnight.

Chapter Five

Why do I only ever want the things that are packed into boxes?

'But, Mum, please, it's my glittery talcum powder – I know which box it's in, I'll get it so quick.'

'No. You don't need the glittery talcum powder now.'

She doesn't know. It could be a matter of life and death. What if I need that or my spirally pen with the fluffy end, or what about my sticker book or goblin mask? I might need these things literally at the drop of a hat.

But no. Instead Mum makes us sit in the garden with triangle sandwiches and juice out of squeezy

boxes to 'keep out the way' while her and Dad load the van. I want to *load the van*. I want to make sure all my precious things get tooked care of properly. I've seen these removal people before, you know, and sometimes they don't think twice about carelessly slinging your objects into the back of a van.

It's boiling hot. I feel tired and more thirsty than the amount of juice in the carton I've got left. I've drained the container so hard the straw is toothy and flattened.

'I BORED,' Hector says. He lies on the grass and

takes the ham out of one of the sandwiches and lies it over his eyes. Gross. 'Look, ha-ha, hamglasses,' he laughs. We have to laugh too.

'I don't want to move house,' Poppy says. 'Once uponed a time a girl from even at my school moved house and her house was actually not a house but . . . a . . . a . . . it was actually a . . .'

Poppy has been lying a lot lately. I am really noticing this. I don't say anything and let her think this one through.

'But actually it was a school.'

'So she moved into a new house and actually it was a school?'

'Yes. And the teachers were all there, locked in prisons, and she had to do tests and exams when she brushed her teeth to go to bed at night.'

'Really?' I play the game and pretend. 'Did they not go to see the house before they bought it?'

'No, because they . . . erm . . . weren't allowed, and also they won the house as a prize on a TV game show.'

I roll my eyes. The lies are so boring.

'Stop lying,' I say.

'I am NOT lying.'

'Yes you are – you keep always doing it these days.'

'NO I DON'T, DARCY!' she screams, which is obviously a clear fact of evidence that she *is* lying.

'If you're gonna lie, at least then make it a good lie, like not some pointless boring lie about nothing.'

'I don't lie. I'm telling Mum all about you.'

'Go on then.'

'Mum will be really mad at you.'

'Mum will be madder at you though, much morer, Poppy, because Mum HATES a tell-tell *snitch*.'

'Yeah, well. It's very important not to make lies up about me lying.'

'I SO BORED!' Hector moans.

Lamb-Beth is sniffing the grass and looking for any misplaced bits of sandwich crumbs. I feel very sorry for animals. Poor Lamb-Beth has absolutely zero idea that we are moving house today! We watch  her in silence. She wees up the fence.

'Why don't we build her a zoo?' Hector asks.

'I HATE zoos!' I shout, all loud.

'Why?' Poppy asks.

'They are animal prisons.'

'What do you mean, *animal prisons*?' Hector whimpers, all shocked.

'Imagine if I said to you, *Hector, you're gonna be locked inside this room all day. For ever.* Not with me. Not with Poppy or Mum or Dad or any of your favourite clothes or games or treats to eat.'

'That's horrible for me!' Hector cries.

'I *used* to like zoos,' Poppy mutters, 'but since that girl at my school went to live in a zoo in the South Pole I never ever liked them, because she said they never fed them any chocolate cake, only apples and worms.'

There goes another lie. She looks to the ground.

'Let's build a den!' Hector suggests.

'Or the funfair again?' Poppy offers.

'We can't, all the bits are packed away.'

'Why don't we make a present for the new people moving into our house?'

'A present? They are getting OUR house, that's such a big present!' Poppy barks.

'We could write them a letter?' I say.

'Yes . . . all about us!' Poppy claps her hands.

'And put it in a box and bury it in the ground?'

'Yes! Like a time capsule!'

'I know . . .' Hector grins. 'We should trick them!'

'Huh? How?' Poppy asks.

'Good idea! We could pretend we are from the past, from the Victorian days?' I shout.

'No, Egypt!' Poppy argues. 'And this house is a pyramid.'

'I think they will know they aren't in Egypt, Poppy.'

Then again, those lies do spread!

'What about the morer future?' Hector's eyes light up. 'We are aliens!'

'You GENIUS!' I laugh out loud. 'That will really totally throw them!' I jump up and down. 'Poppy, you go in and get paper and pens.'

'Why do I have to?'

'Because you're cuter.'

'Can't you ask?'

'No, you ask.'

'Just ask.'

'No, you ask.'

'You just don't want to cos you're scared that Mum is gonna shout at you.'

'No I'm not, you're scared that Mum will shout at YOU, which is why you just said it.'

'No! Not true!'

We are arguing so much that we completely forget that Hector has his rucksack with him which is full of his boring baby colouring-in books and pens. He is already scribbling away.

'Can I write it out?' Poppy asks, holding her hand out for a pen.

'No, me, I want to!' Hector holds the pen tight to his chest.

'Don't fight!' I shout. 'But we might need to make Poppy write, Hector, if we are going to make up a special alien language.'

'Why?'

'Because you and me are the worserest spellers out of the three of us.'

'Yes.' Poppy nods. 'I'm a ten-out-of-ten speller, my teacher said so.'

'Why do we need to spell good?'

'Because if we are going to jumble up the language it needs to be the right language to begin with,' I explain.

''K.' Hector hands a pen to Poppy.

'So let's make like a code then, yeah?'

'Yeah!'

'OK!'

'We have to confuse them and make them think that they have to do silly things!'

We are all laughing as we begin writing the code of our alien language, and then we begin to write . . .

Elloh,

Ew rea liensa romf het uturef!
Ouy illw EVERN eb blea ot
nderstandu uro pecials anguagel
nlessu ouy anc peaks het
anguagel fo het uturef!
Oodg uckl ryingt ot reakb het
odec!

Het eary si 3001! Ew rea a amilyf
fo eniusg liensa hatt ivedl ni hist ouseh nda verye
ayd ew erew ents no OPT ECRETS ISSIONSM yb uro
ommanderc! Uro amesn rea Umm, Add, Arcyd, Oppyp nda
Ectorh. Ew lsoa aveh a etp ambl amedn Ambl-Ethb.

Uro avouritef oodsf rea agicm paces ustd, erealc
ithw ooeyg arshmallowm artianm aval yrups ouredp lla
vero ti. Ew lsoa ate oonm-loudc andwichess, akedb
steroida astap akeb, nda ilkym-ayw heesecakec. Ti si
eryv ommonc ereh ot ate ogd oop. Ni actf fi ouy od otn
RYT atinge ogd oop ta eastl nceo, ouy illw eb ni uiteq

eriouss roublet: cientistss aveh ealrizedr hatt ogd oop si ERYV OODG orf su! Akem ures ot ays Elloh ot oury wen eighboursn. Heyt rea liensa oot! Heyt ate OTSL fo odg oop os ti ightm eb a icen deai ot akeb hemt a ogd-oop akec? Ti si lsoa eryv ormaln ereh ot ipew oury oothbrusht ni xtrae oth hillic auces nda ate yfift arlicg lovesc a ayd.

Thero liensa illw lla eb retendingp ot eb umansh os ti si a eryv oodg deai ot etl hemt niowk uoy rea na liena yb oingd a olyr-olyp ightr yb heirt eetf, ickingl heirt acesf ourf imest nda oingd a hickenc anced. Fi hatt ailsf, hent hrowt a reshlyf ookedc ishf iep vero heirt eadsh, allingc hemt a tupids dioti poons accoonr-acedf widdlemincht nda artingf eallyr oudlyl ni heirt ightr are.

Ot itf ni ereh icelyn, unr rounda het ardeng akedn, aintp oury ouseh ainbowr olouredc nda cta ikel VERYE AYD is OURY irthdayb!

Oodg uckl!

Het Urdocksb!

(To read the original letter without the code turn to the back of the book ☺)

We read the letter back. We are laughing and sniggering so much.

'Kids!' Dad calls. 'You guys ready?'

'Just a minute!' I shout. 'Quick, quick, dig a hole . . .'

'But it will get all soily and damp in the ground,' Poppy says, all worriedly.

'OK . . . push it through the straw hole of the juice carton,' I suggest.

'It's all wetted with apple juice and it looks like rubbish – how will they know there's a letter inside?'

'Oh, yeah. OK . . .'

What can we put it inside?

'Wrap it the sandwich foil.'

'Yeah, that looks spacy and futuristic.' Poppy starts wrapping the letter. 'And then put it in Hector's sock.'

135

'Wait! No! That's my sock!' Hector screeches.

'Yeah, but what's more important? This one sock or this great message pretending we are aliens?'

It's a no-brainer. Hector whips off his striped sock and we begin digging the hole deep in the ground. The earth is dry and crumbles away like biscuit.

'Kids! Come on! You ready?' Mum peeps out and we all quickly turn round with our hands behind our back, hiding our dirty nails.

'Yes, we are just saying a big goodbye to the garden.'

'OK, well come on, the big van is leaving.' She goes back indoors.

Quick, quick, we rake and claw the ground, we use a pen as a spade. Lamb-Beth thinks we are mad. Then, when we've got as far down as we can, we shove the foiled letter inside the striped sock and plant it like a futuristic seed in the ground. We then bury, bury, bury the soil on top, leaving a tincy bit of the sock hanging out as a clue.

We then high-five each other and run into the

house and out into the street to see the van driving away. We are so excited from our secret special letter to be founded we forget to say goodbye to the house. But it's OK – I don't know about you . . . but I've never been any good at goodbyes anyway.

Chapter Six

The door is open as the delivery men are charging in and out like they own the joint. I thought it was going to be all powdery and dusty, like opening an old treasure chest or something, but no. It's as if the people moved out only an hour ago. The rooms look big and stark but luckily the windows are open so the sun is here too. The good old sun, he always knows to show his face when you need him the most . . . Poppy and Hector run off, exploring and touching and prodding and probing but I'm anxious . . . I wonder where all my new thinking spots will be. I find my brain looking for things that are worse about this place compared to our old house rather than better, like how the tap in the kitchen is one big tap rather than separate taps. AND anyway, WHY IS IT ALL SO BIG?

'Where's my Heelies?' Poppy asks Dad.

'Not now, not yet.'

'Oh, please.'

'Not now!'

Poppy doesn't even need them. She can judder down the stairs on her belly or back without Heelies. She runs over to me, smiling. 'The floor is so shiny, if we wanted to we can slide down the banisters, we can swish and scoop and hide and flop and leap and crawl and climb!' she pants. 'There are so many cupboards and new corners! Come on!' She takes my hand and we run around together. The bathrooms are decor- ated much nicer as

Dad did them both up before we moved in as Mum didn't want to wee on an old toilet, or bath in an old bath. We've NEVER had two toilets before.

'We can wee at the same time!' Poppy shouts to me as I look at myself in the too-high-up mirror. 'This can be MY bathroom and that can be *your* bathroom? This one has a shower, see?'

We run. Run. Run.

'And this is MY owned LOVELIEST bedroom!' Poppy announces. 'Look at this window, all mines, and this cupboard and my bed is going here and my rug there and all my Beanie Babies all lined up. Show me your bedroom!'

And I run to find mine, but it's all the other way on the other side of the hall, not as close as what it was before which makes me feel a bit nervous and scared. But when I get in there I see all the boxes say MASTER BEDROOM.

Master?

Me?

I mean, I completely knew I was a complete don of the whole world and absolutely wonderful, but a MASTER? WOW! Chill out, Mum and Dad! But when I peep my eyes in the bags and boxes I see that these aren't my things. These are Mum and Dad's things. I don't own posh perfumes and big clunky leather dompy shoes.

So . . . *this* MUST be my room. I go to the smaller one next to Mum and Dad's. But it's all got boxes with HECTOR writted on the side. He's already in there, swishing his cars about the floor. And then there's the other one . . . ah yes, my room must be . . .

but it's full of Dad's papers and Dad's swishy work chair . . . wait . . . this isn't what we planned . . .

I count. One. Two. Three. Four. *Where's my bedroom?*

And then I see the stairs . . .

'Ah, you've spotted it then?' Mum asks as she blows her hairs out of her eyes, carrying a box with **DARCY** writted on the side.

'What?'

'You've got the attic room.'

'The attic room?'

'Yes . . . like a proper writer. Isn't it amazing? Come and see.'

I gulp. Big. Hard. Like a snake swallowing a whole egg. Up the creaky steep narrow staircase, the walls get lower and lower and then fan up into a triangle shape. Huge beams stalk the ceiling, open and big.

'I thought this
was going to be
Dad's office.'

'No, that's
downstairs now.
We thought this would be for you . . .'
Mum smiles. I hear Dad's feet softly padding
up the stairs too.

'Hey, monkey, what do you reckon then?
Pretty sweet, right?'

'Errrmmmm.'

'Your own space, a view of the river . . .
Look . . . you can almost see the London Eye from
here . . . see?'

'Oh, yeah,' I gulp.

'And I thought you could have a desk here and
your bed here . . . there's plenty of space . . . and
maybe when we get enough saved we could build you
your own bathroom up here too.'

WHAT ARE THEY TRYING TO DO?
Gently move me out? Move me up into the clouds so

they can forget I exist? I don't want to be up here chilling with the ghosts and vampires and spiders. All on my own. All by my own self. With only horror dreams for company.

'So all byed myself?'

'Yes.' Dad grins. 'Isn't it beautiful? Look at these beams – they are original, you know.'

'What if they fall down on my head in the night?'

'They won't.'

'What about if maybe we went back to our other house now?'

Mum laughs. 'Why would you want to do that?' She puts her hands on her hips. 'Don't you like it up here?' Her face goes from a friendly proud smile to suddenly anxious. Worried. Disappointed, even. 'We thought you'd love it up here, D.'

I want to say, *You're right.* You are absolutely right, Mum and Dad. But I don't think I will like it up here because it's big and scary and dark and it's away from everybody else and it feels too far away and growed up and forgotted about.

Then I think about my trying-not-to-be-dramatic challenge and I can see my parents' faces, both eagerly nodding, and I say, 'It's perfect. I love it. Thank you so much.'

We wave goodbye to the removal men and Dad gives them extra money than they even asked for and I don't know why. You don't give extra money to the person behind the counter at the supermarket, do you? Anyway, I'm glad those men are gone because one of them had a smell from their armpits that was like a burger fryer. Gross.

Back downstairs the sunshine leaps in huge slanted golden triangles and squares, and dusty particles spiral through the air. We whip tape off boxes and reunite with our packed-away belongings. Objects look different a bit. Dirtier. Stranger. Smaller. Dad wires the speakers up and puts music on and it patters all around the house in the familiar echoey voice of our favourite David Bowie, but it doesn't sound all how it sounded in our old house. The walls are all cold even though it's summer and it smells funny in my room.

Like old air freshener and dust. And other strange people.

Dad comes up and drills my bed together. It's a double bed now. Apparently this is something I should be feeling so excited about. But I feel nervous. Even though I asked for one.

Dad has a smear of sweat on his brow but he's got a cold beer and is singing along to Bowie. He is really *into* this moving malarkey. Watching my bed get all drilled up only makes the chances of me not having this as my bedroom less and less. The fact that this is where I will spend the rest of my life growing becomes realer with every turn of every screw. Is it too late to have his office as my room? Is it too late to swap?

'How brilliant is it here, D?' Dad opens his arms to take it all in, wobbling the bed to make sure the bolts are all tight. They are. *Sadly*.

'Brilliant,' I whisper.

'Right, better do Princess Poppy's bed, then!' He squeezes the trigger of the drill and cackles. Absolutely *lovin' life*. He swigs his beer and clambers down my rickety staircase. The rickety staircase that no one will ever climb up. The stairs that are easy to forget about.

I begin unpacking. I line my books up all nice and tidy on the shelves. Mum says that books are the best ornament in the world and can make any house a *home*. So I'm hoping that feeling will come to me soon. In the wardrobe I hang all my clothes, which look silly and childish. All the colours are too shouty and brash and bold. Bleugh. I never used to find these clothes too silly, so why do I think they look so odd and out of place now? Why does everything feel out of place? Perhaps it's because Lamb-Beth isn't up here? Let me go and fetch her.

I tumble downstairs. Already I feel sick. EVERY-BODY is on this floor. Mum's sorting out Hector's room, Hector is putting his toys away and making a sign for his door, Poppy is sticking her posters on the wall and Dad is building up her bed. I watch them all for a minute. Doing Burdock life without me. Where do I fit in in ALL this then, eh?

I barge myself into Poppy's room.

'How's it going?' I ask.

'Absolutely SO amazing. I love my big room. Look at it!'

'Where's Lamb-Beth?' I ask, ignoring her showy-offy annoyingness, and her being all settled like petals around a flower.

'She's sleeping here. I found her waiting at the bottom of the staircase up to your room – she can't get up.'

'What do you mean she can't get up?'

'She couldn't climb up the slippy steep staircase. She was bleating and crying.'

'Huh?' I shake my head and scoop her up. This can't be. I can't have my own main friend Lamb-Beth not being able to come up and visit me whenever she wishes. I try to grab her up.

'Well, I will just have to train her to get up to me then, won't I?' I say. 'We can't be having that?'

'Leave her alone,' Dad says. 'Let her sleep – look how tired she is.' His eyes focus on drilling Poppy's bedpost. 'Go back up there and finish putting your things away.'

Oh. Right. I see. Don't worry then, guys. I'll just go BACK UP THERE. Is that what it's always going to be like from now on then? *Go back up there, Darcy?* Like I'm some horrid haggled stumpy hunchback that has to live in a bell-tower attic. Oh, I get it. Don't you worry. I get it.

So I turn round and gather my thoughts by *going back up there* to my pit. I charge, Lamb-Beth-less, up the narrow, steep, crooked, slippy stairs, but I lose my footing and slip, trip, bang my head, stupid sweaty soles of stupid feet send me flying up like I have butter on my heels, and BANG – knock my tooth and my nose – BOOF! BANG! OUCH. Bruise. I can taste jammy bitter metal bean-canny blood. Face is all purple already and I begin to get all teary and I want to scream and cry but I just howl in deep private, and

instead of being all so dramatic I just don't. I pick myself up and climb myself up the stairs even though I feel like Sara Crewe in *A Little Princess*, all banished to the attic, and I raid every upturned box and bag until I find my writing book and I write.

DEAR MRS HAY,

YOU ARE SO ANNOYING.

I HATE THIS TASK BECAUSE I AM NOT MYSELF. I AM A DRAMATIC GIRL. THAT IS WHO I AM. I AM A DRAMATIC TYPE OF PERSON, SO DEAL WITH IT. I AM NEVER JUST HUNGRY – I AM *STARVING*. I AM NEVER JUST THIRSTY – I AM *PARCHED*. I AM NEVER JUST TIRED – I AM *EXHAUSTED*. THAT IS WHO I AM. YES, I MIGHT MOAN AND MOAN AND MAKE A SMALL MOLEHILL INCIDENT INTO A HUGE EVEREST MOUNTAIN. YES, WHEN I CRY A FEW TEARS I MIGHT SAY THAT I

CRIED *AN OCEAN.* BUT WHEN I LOVE
SOMETHING I LOVE IT *TO DEATH.*
AND WHEN I LAUGH — I LAUGH MY
HEAD UNTIL IT ROLLS OFF. AND
WHEN I'M HAPPY I'M ACTUALLY OVER
THE REAL MOON ELATED. AND WHEN
SOMETHING TOUCHES ME — IT CUTS
LIKE A KNIFE. YES, I AM A BIG PIECE
OF WORK, YES, I AM A BIG BITE,
YES, I AM A LOT TO CHEW. I AM *A*
LOT. BUT I *LOVE* THAT ABOUT ME. I
AM FULLY BAKED. I AM FULLY LOADED.
I AM THE REAL DEAL. I AM NOT
BORING. I AM 100% AND MORE.
I AM ME.

I write so hard my hand feels so sore because
I've dug the pen so deep into the paper and I feel
the real urge to run down to Mum and be honest
and say I hate this stupid challenge and I'm scared

about my new room and I'm terrified of sleeping in here and Lamb-Beth can't even climb the stairs and actually neither can I because I just fell over on them, but then I hear the doorbell ring . . .

It's a funny sound. Our new doorbell.

And it's Dad's voice saying the best words that make everything OK for a minute . . .

'Pizza's here!'

Chapter Seven

Both Hector and Poppy couldn't WAIT to sleep in their new rooms. But I was hoping that Mum and Dad would just simply forget that I had a bedtime as I lay curled up as a silent mouse on the corner of the couch. I was hoping they'd forget that I had to go *back up there*. And find me a new room, somewhere else in the new house. But they didn't. And eventually they did see me.

'Right, come on, bedtime, monkey nut.' And oh, how I wanted to grumble and groan, but knew

Squeak Squeak

I couldn't because of my NO DRAMA challenge. 'We'll come tuck you in in a bit.' I was tired from the long day and the unpacking and the smack of summer and the hot cheesy pizza fullness swelling in my belly so maybe I'd just roll off to sleep.

But in bed, I can hear Mum and Dad softly laughing in Poppy's room. So she obviously wasn't asleep but she seemed so happy. I could hear them all sounding so relaxed and over the moon, their bassy tones rattling up my wooden beams. They are there for ages and ages and ages. HELLLLOOOOO? Thought they were coming to see me? I've started to think that there might not be any ghosts in this house after all . . . because it's me who is the ghost!

I hear the crunchy crackle of soft footing on wooden stairs. Mum and Dad's little voices all roomy and glad and I don't know why I do it. I crinkle my eyes shut and pretend to be asleep. I drop my breathing really low and quiet and try not to make my eyelids shake.

'Ah, look,' Mum sighs. 'She must be exhausted, tired thing.'

Mum strokes my hair and they both kiss me on the cheeks.

'She'll be happy up here,' Dad whispers. 'Come on now, don't wake her.'

And I want to splash up out of bed and shout, 'NOOOOOO! DON'T GO. DON'T LEAVE ME! PLEASE . . . I'M JUST YOUR LITTLE GIRL.' But I don't. They click the light off and plunge me into darkness as the sound of their footsteps move further and further away . . .

In the dark all my actions are extra-large in the attic. Every sound I seem to do feels walloping and huge. I keep needing a wee but having to hold it in. I must be brave. And growed up. And not at all dramatic. Fumbling about, lost, in the new navy blue blackness. I will NEVER be able to race the flush of the toilet to get back upstairs to bed in this new room before it finishes flushing. Not never.

The whole house is so quiet and still and uncertain. I lie, eyes up at the ceiling in the blank darkness. The

room's high beams seem to grow in front of me, like a never-ending abyss. I feel as close to the sky as space. Like I am in space. My pupils dilate in the dark. My bed is so big and swallowing. Easily an alien or a monster could wriggle in with me and I wouldn't even know it. A giant could shove his nose through the window, eyes peering. WAH! I clench my eyes shut up tight. I don't dare touch the empty side of the bed where the sheets are all cold and the fabric is so soft and still. I just stay completely locked to my side, like a coffin. Not moving one bit. I am grain-of-sand small.

The creaky old house begins to murmur and groan and mumble like the entire place is a body with a belly-ache. I hear all the new noises . . . the pipes that clank and chop and scratch like little hamsters are running around them. I feel so cold, like I'm in a shed . . . it feels SO cold like the Arctic snowstorm and the wind whistles and blows through every creak and cranny. But I know outside it's summertime hot, and I start to sweat.

I wish my bed was all pushed up to the wall like

before. I want the comfort of the surface behind my back. I want to feel my breath touching the wall. My eyes are crimped so tight shut. I suddenly remember that I lost a pair of knickers down behind the radiator in my old bedroom and never remembered to fish them out. They will still be there now. Taking it so personally that I forgot them. I KNEW I'd forget them. Now somebody else will find them. CRINGE. How embarrassing.

I begin to get scared of all the unknown things that I don't want to find in this new house. I don't want to find some old sock or knickers belonging to somebody else behind the radiator. Some horrible reminder left over from a body that lived here in your very own house before you. *Bleugh.*

A tear maybe slips out of my eye. I wouldn't say it was a real-life tear, but I'm not 100% sure. And I am so cross at Poppy in her cosy pink princess paradise and Hector in his lovely toy room. And Mum and Dad have each other. It's not fair that when you get older you get to share a room again with a person

– it's the wrong way round, because when you get older you get braver, so if anything THAT is when you should have to start sleeping on your own. Not now. Being just a small child still. I wish Lamb-Beth was here. I wish I wasn't on my own. I wish the room wasn't so big and the ceiling so high and the pipes so clanky and cranky and the windows so howly and the moon so silent, and then I hear footsteps . . .

Creep. Creep. Creep. *No. Oh, what now?* Please, not a ghost. Please, not a monster. Please, not a killer. Please, no . . . I can't be bothered to die. Or be scared. Not now, please . . .

The figure begins to move closer and closer and closer . . . I can feel the breath of it, curling over the edge of me, as it towers, warmer, warmer . . . warm . . .

'Darcy.' It's Poppy's whisper. 'It's scary in my room. Can I sleep with you?'

And then I have to make one of those big live decisions that only a big sister can truly make . . . to be honest and say I was scared too, and say how happy I am to see her, or . . .

'Oh, sorry, I was just sleeping,' I awful lie/pretend as if she's rudely woked me up. 'Yes, of course you can.' And then I wink to myself as we snuggle into each other, hands holding, and immediately can fall asleep. It isn't long before I hear more footsteps coming up my stairs, this time a little lighter, a little softer, and then Hector's voice, softly saying, 'I scared, can I get in too?'

Chapter Eight

Week 3/6

Although the house still isn't completely feeling like ours entirely yet we are feeling much more betterer about things. Poppy and Hector have been sleeping upstairs in the attic with me every night and Dad says he knew that double bed would come in handy. He thinks it's funny that even though we've moved somewhere bigger, us three have still all stayed glued to each other in the same bed, like *three peas in a pod*. Which is exactly what we are. Even though we actually have our own pods.

We have been in our house for exactly one week and it is week three of the holidays! Mum said that now things have settled after 'living under a rock' for a bit and 'everything being everywhere' we are allowed to choose something fun to do today.

YES!

It's narrowed down to a list like this:

Go to a chocolate factory

Go to the wild jungle

Go to watch WWE wrestling in real life

Go go-karting

Go to a real waterfall

Go underwater in a submarine

Go into the sky in a rocket — will settle for an air balloon as long as it's a quick one and not baby-snail slow

Go to a water park

Meet a sick snake

Dye my hair blue

Go on a comic-making course

Be locked in a newsagent's overnight with the freedom to eat all the crisps I want without anybody judging me

But every time I'm trying to show Mum the list she seems to be busy now.

'Mum, Mum, I've thought about it, I've thought about *what I'd like to do today*.'

'Hang on a moment, chicken monkey.'

Grrrrrrr.

'Mum, but you said to think about what to do today and I thought about it.'

'What about Poppy and Hector?'

'They are happy with the list too.'

'Pass it here.' She quickly skates her eyes across the letters. 'OK, so you expect me to believe that Hector would like to dye his hair and that Poppy would like to meet a *sick snake* . . . whatever that is?'

'Mum, you've been ages at the computer now, come on.'

'Can't you guys just play amongst yourselves for a bit while I do these last few bits.'

'You said that ages ago.'

'Darcy!' she snaps.

'You *said*.'

Great.

I guess as I'm the most olderest one it's up to me to think of an activity.

'Right,' I say to Poppy and Hector as I proudly enter the living room, 'I've got a good idea.'

'OK, what is it?'

'We are going to make a bath in the shower.'

'Huh?'

We never had a proper shower in the old house. Not one with a door like a cubicle. I was thinking about it while I was weeing the other day. I looked at the cubicle and I thought, *It must be possible to make that into a swimming pool.* I have a clear vision of us floating at the top, the depth of the whole shower being one long cylinder of water! We could put bubbles in and pretend to be scuba divers!

In our swimsuits we all pile into the shower. I turn the shower on and freezing cold water splashes out.

'Quick, quick, move to the wall,' Poppy orders the team, squealing.

'It's going to warm up in a sec,' I reassure them.

'Aargh, that's more betterer,' Hector giggles.

'OK, what now?' Poppy asks.

'Is the shower door properly shut?' I ask.

'Yep.'

'Eugh, did you just wee down my leg?' I ask Poppy.

'Sorry, I couldn't help it.' She shrugs.

'Keep your wee over to that side.'

'Water is just going all down the plug hole, why won't it just stay?' Hector asks, disappointed.

'Block the drain, we need a plug,' says Poppy in a fluster.

'The shower doesn't have a plug,' says me, obvs,

cos I am the oldest and know that, duh.

'OK, pass the plug from the sink,' Poppy says to Hector.

Hector leaps out all wet and reaches into the sink on his tiptoes. 'It has a beady necklace thing on it.'

'Break it off,' Poppy says.

'That's naughtily.' Hector blushes, his eyes all wide.

'Mum told us to make our own fun, so that's what we're doing, don't be boring,' I reassure him.

'Ouch, I just nearly slipped.' Hector judders forward.

'Be careful.'

'Let me.' Poppy gets out, all wet, and goes to help him with the sink plug. The warm spray of the shower is galloping all over my back.

'You're getting splashes all everywhere,' I say as I watch them.

'You do it then if you think you're so good,' Poppy bites back. 'The plug necklace won't come off the sink.'

'Pull harder,' I offer.

'I am.'

'Oh. Let me try. Pass it here.'

Chink.

'There we go.' I hold the plug up.

'YES!'

'Looks too small,' Poppy
says after all the hard
effort.

'Let's try it.'

'Move your feet,
Hector.'

'You're bad.' Hector bites his lip, concerned that
we are going to go to prison for this.

'It's too small.'

'Told you.'

'Let me try and—'

'No, that won't stay. Pass me that cup,' I say,
engineering a new plug.

'That's my cup,' Hector cries back.

'Shut up.' Poppy taps his arm.

'Pass the sponge, then.'

'Maybe we can . . . does that look covered?'

'I think, yes.' Hector gets excited again and claps his hands. 'Is the water filling up?'

'Dunno, close the door more tight. Block the bottom bit.'

'With what?' Poppy looks around, the water still drumming onto our heads.

'Your fingers,' I order.

'Oh, look, Darcy, it's filling up!' Poppy squeals.

'Aargh, it's gonna be so tall!' Hector jumps up, elated.

'And deep!' Poppy adds. 'Like a fish tank!'

'Oh no.'

'It's going all downed the plughole again.'

'Oh.'

'It doesn't work.'

'And we broked the sink chain.' Hector looks down and whispers to himself.

'Let's get out.' Poppy already leaves the shower, trying to pretend she wasn't involved at all.

'Did you bring in a towel?' I ask.

'No. Did you?'

'OK, quick then, you get out of the way then and I'll go and get one,' I offer.

'Can't we all go?'

Blip. Blop. Drip. Drop. Splish. Splosh. Splash. Wet Darcy, Poppy and Hector footprint shapes are marked all the way around the landing.

After we dry off we have to think of something else to do next, to not let boredom interfere our lives and ruin us.

'I know,' Hector says, 'let's make a secret den.'

'They never work good.' Poppy shakes her head.

'OK. I know,' I say.

'What?'

'Let's jump off the wardrobe?' I suggest.

'OK.'

'Land on Mum's bed!'

'OK!'

'And when you land you have to say something!'

'OK, and when you get to the top of the wardrobe you have to say something too!' Poppy says with a naughty face on.

'Like . . . a swear word?' Hector shows his teeth.

'No! Not a swear word, you'll be in trouble.'

'Like BUM BUM!' Hector screams. 'BUMS AWAY!'

'KIDS!' Mum shouts. 'Kids! Stop making a racket.'

'Shh.' Poppy puts her finger over her mouth.

'You shhh.' Hector puts his own finger over Poppy's mouth.

'Can't you ask Mum's permission to jump?' Poppy asks me.

'You ask,' I snap back.

'No, *you* ask.'

'Why can't you just ask?'

'I know. Why don't we go down the stairs with Mum's skirt on – because look, it's so shiny, this one will just shimmy down so smoothly, won't it?' Poppy raids Mum's wardrobe.

'Yes, I can wear this one – look, it's velvet, so soft. I'll put this one on.' Hector picks out a skirt while picking his own nose.

'Don't make a mess, she will see we've been through her things,' I say as I see a crispy bogey of his already nestling on the fabric.

'I'm not making a— Look at this.'

'Oh yes, that's so smooth.'

'There's no more silky skirts – what can I wear?' I ask.

'Hmmm . . . has Dad got a thing you can wear?' Poppy suggests as she wriggles into Mum's posh skirt. 'What about the guitar case?'

'HA! Yes, it's all floppy and leathery, like a mermaid tail.'

'Yes. You can tuck your legs in!'

'Like a seal!'

'Ha!'

Bounce. Bounce. Bounce. Waddle. Waddle. Waddle.
Hop. Hop. Hop.

''K, Hector go first,' Poppy bosses.

'Ouch, you're on my skirt!' Hector shrieks.

'Hector *loves* that skirt.'

'No I don't!'

'OK, go!'

'Poppy said I *love that skirt.*'

'No, I didn't mean it.'

'You said it.'

'Just go now.'

'Say sorry.'

'No, there's no real need to say sorry. It was a joke. You need to learn to take a joke.' Poppy clamps her arms around Hector's tummy.

'Oh, Hector, stop being silly and just slide down the stairs.' I rub his shoulder.

'Not until Poppy says sorry.'

'I'm not saying sorry, Hector, because I said nothing wrong.'

'SAY IT!' Hector roars.

'Poppy, just say sorry,' I usher, nudging her stubbornness.

'No, I didn't do anything wrong.'

'Come on, this is getting long now.'

'Fine, *sorry*.' Poppy rolls her eyes. 'There, said it, OK?'

'OK,' Hector reluctantly accepts.

'Not really. Now go!' Poppy howls, and she pushes Hector down the stairs in the skirt.

'AARGH!' he cries.

'Poppy!' I scold.

'You shoved me,' Hector whimpers.

'Cos you're holding us up!'

'I wasn't ready.'

Bunk. Plunk. Bunk. Plunk. Klunk. Jabbbbbbbberrrr. Jabbbbbbberrrrr. AARGGGGGGGHHHHHHH!!!

'Move! Move! I'm right behind you!'

Bunk. Plunk. Bunk. Plunk. Klunk. Jabbbb-bbb-be-blump. BASH. CRASH. BUMP.

'MOVE! YOU TWO! OUT THE WAY!'

Blump. Blump. Thump. Bash. Bish. Thump.

'Ow! My head.'

'My finger bent back, got stuck in this stupid anorak toggle hanging on the banister.'

'Let's do it again.'

'Really?'

'OK, this time Darcy go first, so if there's a pile-up, at least she is biggest and we can use her like a crash pad,' Poppy bosses us about some more.

''K. Get up then,' I agree, trying not to be offended by the idea of being a human crash pad.

'Jeez, this skirt is so long it's all getting wrapped up around my feet and you're stepping on it.'

'Sorry.'

'Lift up your foot, lift— No, not that one.'

'I am.'

'That one.'

RIIIIIIIIIIIIIIIIP. TEAR. BURST. RIP.
CRISSSSSSSSSSSSSH.

'Oh no.'

'Oh.'

'Mum's skirt. It's ripped.'

'No.'

'Tored.' Hector points.

'Poppy!'

'Wasn't my fault,' Poppy
defends herself, as usual.
'You stepped on it,' she blames.
'Quick . . .' She has an idea.

'What?'

'Hide it upstairs.'

'Where?' I ask.

'Back of her wardrobe.'

'We can't do that.' I chew the inside of my mouth.

I know how much Mum loves that skirt, it's a special precious-occasion one.

'Shove it in the bin,' Poppy says.

'We can't. It's a posh Mum skirt.'

'Don't cry, Poppy,' says Hector.

'It was a mistake.'

'Try and sew it back.' I rub her shoulder in support but in a *I'm so glad this is you and not me* position.

'I can't sew.'

'We don't have *any* skills.'

'I hate this about us.'

'Buy a new one.'

'I've never even heard of this design.' Poppy collapses onto the ground.

'And we have no money.'

'Call Dad.'

'Say what?'

'That we are sorry but we broke Mum's skirt.'

'Mum will hear.'

'Hide it in the washing basket. Wipe poo on it and say she did it,' Hector offers.

'I think she would know if she pooed on her skirt and threw it in the washing basket.'

'I know . . .' Poppy gets new energy: she has thought of something else.

'What?'

'We will play shops, yeah?'

'Yeah?'

'Invite Mum to look around the shop, and then when she picks up her skirt, pretend to fall over and say *MUM! YOU RIPPED IT!*'

'That's very bad.' Hector shakes his head.

'Blame Lamb-Beth,' Poppy tries again.

'No, *not* blame Lamb-Beth,' I argue. 'She's a very *good* girl.'

'Somebody has to be blamed for this.'

'Yeah, but who?'

And then we hear the door knock and the familiar screechy voice of Marnie Pincher: 'COOOO-EEE!'

'KIDS!' Mum shouts. 'Guess who's popped over?'

And we can't help but smile. The afternoon is about to get better . . .

Chapter Nine

'I want to see the money before I do it.'

'A dare doesn't work like that, Donald,' I argue.

'Why do you always love money so much anyway?' Poppy rightly snubs.

'Money represents trust! My dad told me so!' EYEBALL-ROLL TO THAT. He continues, 'How do I know to trust you? I wouldn't trust me after I lied about you guys in the garden.'

'*THAT* was a very long time ago now, Donald. We are willing to forget.'

'OK, so all I have to do is put the skirt on and jump off the wardrobe?'

'Yeah!' I say, as though it's just a bit of harmless fun.

'And shout something when you do it!' Poppy instructs, which isn't actually necessary but I guess makes it seem less like organized crime.

'Shout something like what?' Donald asks with his no-imagination mind.

'Dunno. Something, anything, whatever.'

'OK. Why do I have to wear the skirt?' he asks innocently. I'd ask the same question.

'It's part of the dare.'

'Whatever. I'm sure you three freaks have your reasons.'

'It matches your black eyes, Donald,' I joke.

'No thanks to you.'

'You're the clumsy one,' I reply.

'Which reminds me, has this thing been tested for injury? It's quite a drop.'

'Yes, we jump off it all the time.' Poppy brushes it off.

'I don't believe you – look at the distance from the wardrobe to the bed.'

'I show you.' Hector nods and clambers up the chair, onto the bookcase and up on top of the

wardrobe. When he reaches the top, he spreads his legs apart and screams, 'BUMS AWAY!'

Crash-landing in the softness of Mum and Dad's bed.

We all laugh. Especially Donald.

'That was great! OK, my turn!' Donald, giggling in snorts, squeezes Mum's skirt up his eggy-shaped body, yanking it up himself. I look to Poppy because that is just perfect. We need Mum's skirt to squeeze around him. The rip is clear for all to see but Donald is too excited to notice. *HA!* We've stitched him up PROPER!

Now, excitedly, holding Mum's ripped skirt all bunched in his hands, Donald begins to crawl up the chair. He looks like a baby in a nappy. He drags himself up the bookcase, which wobbles, a few books tumble off. 'Whoopsy daisy, hold yer horsies, don't want to lose my footing.'

We try not to laugh as he treads carefully over to the wardrobe. It quivers under the weight of him as Donald tries to find his balance. Sticking his arms out he shouts, 'SOMETIMES I STILL WET THE BED BECAUSE I CAN'T BE BOTHERED TO GO TO THE TOILET!'

And we all laugh so hard, so hard that Donald doesn't jump because he's laughing *that* hard. *Snort. Snort.* Like a big pig. *Snout. Snort. Dribble.* Snot pours out of his nose and we laugh harder. All of us. At Donald laughing and snotting with green dribble bubbling out of his nose, with two black eyes and Mum's skirt on, standing on top of the wardrobe shouting about how he sometimes wets the bed! *Howl. Howl. Hooo. Hooo. Ha-ah-ha.*

And then . . .

Three. Two. One . . .

The unexpected, worse detected thing happens that could've happened.

The wardrobe breaks. Completely collapses right underneath Donald.

AARGHHHHHHHHHHHHHH!

CRASH. BANG. BAM. BOOF. CRACK. CREAK. SPLIT. WHACK!

It all happens so quickly. There's the pile of broken wardrobe. The clothes all in piles. Crushed fabric and hangers, like a car-crash tangle of wood and material.

I laugh a bit more. From shock. Then I feel sick. So sick. Because I know what's coming.

Mum's footsteps are banging up the stairs.

'POPPY!' she screams. 'Poppy!'

Huh? Why is she so bothered about Poppy right now?

Mum is not gonna care one bit about her skirt now that her wardrobe is smashed. We are all gonna get so told off about everything. No more jumping off the wardrobe. No more playing. No more fun.

She runs into her bedroom just exactly as Donald emerges, his fat thumb-shaped head sticking up from the rubble.

'HA-HA-HA-HA-HA! What a *blast*!' He dribbles dizzily and we want to laugh more but that just isn't an option right now as Mum spins into the room.

'What *THE*—'

I guess it *is* a lot to take in.

'Is this some kind of joke?' she asks. Staring at us in a gawp, waiting for an answer. Marnie, obviously, has to pop her head round the door too now. Obviously it would be just TOO much to ask to not have her sticking her nosy beak in.

'I do NOT believe what I am seeing!' she crows like the nosy wosy parker she is. Her stiff little plucked eyebrows like two sleeping rats growl into a frown.

I look at Donald, waiting for him to point the finger and blame us for absolutely everything. But he can't keep it together.

He is laughing so hard, and that big dummy grin of his is just shining under the two heavy moons of black

eyes above it. I can't help it. I just get the proper giggles, *hard*. So do Poppy and Hector. Donald looks so ridiculous and finds the whole thing so hilarious. We are all trying to hold the laughter in like an overpacked suitcase filled to the brim and the zip is just gently unzipping, the seams are gently falling apart, thread by thread like . . .

Zzzzzzz . . . zzzzz . . . sssssssss . . . ssssss . . . eeeeee . . . ooooo . . . hhheeeeeee . . . sssssstttttt . . .

And the more we hear each other's suitcase threads of laughter coming apart, we just have to give in to the uncontrollable stuffed-down enormous, belly-aching joy. The more we know we shouldn't be laughing, the more we cannot stop. It's uncontrollable. I might never stop laughing. EVER! Marnie's ratty frowning eyebrows and folded arms are just making it worse, the closeness of us all side by side is just making it worser and worserer! Even with Mum's straight face right there glaring at us. Focus. Focus. Breathe. Breathe. And again . . .

TEE-HEE-TEE-SHHHHH-HA-HEE-OO-

SHH-HA-HAPSHSSSH-HA-HE-TEE-HA-HA-HA-TEE-HEE!

Hands on thighs now, I just have to give in. My tummy muscles release as I cannot clench any longer. All seized up into a big ball.

Wooooo. HHHHHAAAAAAAA. EEEEEEEEEE. OK. OK. *Breathe. I'm fine. I'm fine. Sorry. Sorry.*

I try to get my breath back as Donald clambers up from the heap of clothes.

'Wait . . . is that my vintage silk skirt?' Mum suddenly asks.

'There's a giant rip in it!' Marnie adds.

UH-OH.

'GO TO YOUR ROOMS NOW! I DON'T EVEN WANT TO LOOK AT YOU!' Mum screams.

See, THIS is what I mean? I don't look for it. Drama just A L W A Y S finds me.

DRAMA ALWAYS FINDS ME

If I could, then I would
Live my life in a little box.
I'd paint it white, locked up tight,
Hiding from the sparks of shock.
No fire, no blades,
No dodgy microwaves.
No leaky taps,
Or old mousetraps,
Or trapdoors under doormats. Err. (NO WAY!)
No paper's bad news
To report the blues,
Nothing scary on the TV.
A cereal-full tummy,
And not a coin of money,
To live a life of drama free!
No pets to befriend,
So no need to pretend
I'd like to be dog-walking today.
No friends to depend on,

Less drama to take on,
Narrowing the chances of a wretched surprise
    party!

I'll sleep on a cotton-wool cloud of peace
Where the clocks tick right and leaves scatter in
    the breeze
The grass is green
Blue is the sea
YES, NO
OFF, ON
JUST LIKE A MACHINE.
No elastic, magnetic, fantastic adventure of a
    dream,
No friend to clap hands with
To do it like a team.
I must repress all need to make mess and
    celebrate being free.

Run around colour blind
In a tunnel-vision mind

Where I can't see what is
AMAZING and what is just fine.
In the collar of my coat
I sink my words into my throat,
I shrink myself into a ball
And roll away from it all.
Home. Home. Home.

Shadows spindling on the wall
Looking-glass spider tall.
The cuckoo clock chirps
It's time for tea,
But the kettle explodes
And the jam is just a jar of
   bumble bees

AHHHHHHHHHHHHHH!

And everyone knows . . .

AND YOU CAN'T SPREAD BUMBLE BEES
ON YOUR TOAST!

A horse chips his hoof,

The sunshine falls into the roof,

Baby sick on the bus,

Fall over in the mud,

New trousers flecked in blood,

Who are you talking to?

YOU!

The oven's on

The iron's on

You've grown a set of claws

And your nose is sore – turning into a wicked

   witch again . . . OH NO, NOT AGAIN!

Call a friend – oh, wait, I don't have any . . .

So, for help, you knock on a neighbour's door

But they don't live there any more

And the cat's name is

*Fifigoogoo rice crispy cake with a topping of
salad dressing* and only gets spoken to when
you address her by her complete full name and
say it in a strong *New* Zealand-ish accent.

Which you can't do!

That's LIFE for you!

The roads are made of rubber,

Melting from the summer,

And the cars are

zigzagging and crashing,

But they burst and bounce

like balloons

And the world is moving

like a soft fuzzy cartoon

And you've tried to deny it

But you know that it's true

And you've tried to run from it

But it knows where to come to.

It doesn't matter where you go or what you try

and do . . .

DRAMA ALWAYS FINDS YOU.

Chapter Ten

'I cannot believe you.'

'Sorry, Mum.'

'Sorry doesn't cut it this time.'

'Sorry again, Mum.'

'Not only is my wardrobe broken. My skirt is *ripped*. I don't know which one of you thought it would be funny to let Donald wear my skirt.'

'Not me, Mum,' Poppy says.

'Or me, Mum,' I say.

'Or me either, Mum,' Hector says, even though he probably doesn't even know what he's saying, he's just copying us.

Poppy wraps her little hand into Mum's. She does

this trickly thing where she winds her fingers up Mum's sleeve and strokes her veins when she knows she's been naughty. 'It was all Donald, Mum. Blame Donald,' she says, stroking Mum's hair as Mum sits at the table with a mug of tea. (That I made her.)

'So Donald just went in and took my skirt and just got the urge to put it on, did he, then?'

'Maybe, Mum, yeah?' Poppy says all softly.

'Yeah, maybe,' I add.

'Yeah, maybe he just likes to be a girl?' Poppy offers, shrugging. I want to laugh my head off.

'Are you actually, seriously, considering laughing again?'

'No, Mum.'

'Then after ALL that, what else do I see?'

'I don't know, Mum.'

'You don't know what else I might've seen?'

'No, Mum.'

'Maybe was it that we really broke the plug?' Hector asks innocently.

'You broke the— WHAT?'

'I mean, not really.'

'What plug?'

'It wasn't a true thing what I said.'

'Well, you've said it now. Which plug, Hector?'

'HECTOR! YOU'RE SUCH A BIG MOUTH!' Poppy roars.

'Poppy, you're already in trouble.'

'Darcy pulled it!'

I stay calm. Don't want to be in trouble. Trying not to be dramatic. For minimum punishment (or chances of breaking my promise of being not dramatic for the entire summer holidays) just keep your ears opened and your mouth closed and talk when spoked to. Like ZACTLY like you're in the army.

'Is this true, Darcy?'

'Maybe, Mum, but it's only because I wanted to make a swimming-pool bath in the shower,' I justify myself.

'A swimm— This is ridiculous. So that will obviously explain the three sets of soaking wet footprints running all up and down the hallway and all the water on the bathroom floor?'

Silence.

'Wouldn't it?'

Silence.

'Wouldn't it?' Mum shakes her head. 'I mean, how much chaos can the three of you cause in one day?'

'Chill out, Mum.'

'Darcy. Do NOT tell me to *chill* out.'

'You said we could do something fun today but we never did so that's why we had to make our own fun up.'

'I had to work.'

'You and Dad *always* have to work.'

'Oh, sorry that every day is not circus fun and ice skating and disco balls.' Mum clenches her head. Paces about. Pours a LARGE glass of wine for herself. It's not even dinner time yet. 'Clean this place up now.'

'We're hungry.'

'Oh, I'll just knock up dinner as well as getting Dad to make us a new wardrobe – which we all know will take him *for ever* to make, and then I'll be sorting my clothes and picking them up off the floor and cleaning the carpet and fixing the plug and all the spilled water and everything else you leave around, then?'

'You didn't need to do a list.'

'You didn't need to tell Donald to jump off the wardrobe.'

'I . . .' I want to argue back and say STOP BLAMING US and moan about HOW BORED WE ARE even though it's illegal to be bored and IF she had taken us out like she PROMISED then we wouldn't be in this mess, but, 'Nothing,' I add. I bite my tongue. I trap my mouth shut. Pretend it's full up with chocolate spread or tissue. DO NOT ARGUE BACK. DO NOT BE DRAMATIC. BE CALM AND A GOOD EXCELLENT GIRL.

Tidying away is so bore. I am not good at it. Every time I turn round there is more things to be cleaned. Lamb-Beth does nothing except stare at us from her plumped-up queen cushion like some writer from luxurious heaven and I am just a slave servant beast with a broom. Except I don't have a broom.

'How comes you just kept your temper down then, Darcy?' Poppy asks as we begin to nicely fold up Mum's clothes into some pile on her bed that we don't actually know will even be useful to her or not. 'Usually you'd be so mad right now. You'd be shouting at Mum and everything.'

'I'm still doing my not-dramatic thing, aren't I?'

'You're doing good at that actually,' she says, 'cos if I heard Mum scream YOUR name in panic and not mine when she was running up the stairs I'd be SO jealous.'

'What do you mean, *my* name?'

'Obviously, don't you remember?' Poppy smugly folds the clothes – she thinks she's so good like she works in a shop or something amazing. 'When she heard the wardrobe crash, she ran up the stairs and she was shouting *POPPY! POPPY! POPPY!*'

'So what? What does that mean?'

'Darcy! Oh, silly billy, you really don't know? It's obvious.'

Even Hector stops doing absolutely nothing and looks round now to listen to Poppy.

'Mum was shouting my name because she was worried I'd hurt myself. She was ALL the way downstairs and she heard a bang and she ran up all panicky and she had a choice of three names she could shout, and it was mine. She was most worried that I'd hurted myself. And you know what that means, don't you?'

'No. What?'

'It means Mum loves me the most.'

UP TO MY ROOM! GROWL! HOWL! GRRRRRRRR!

I feel like a locked-up beast in an attic dungeon. I kick a book. I can destroy ANYTHING and EVERYTHING any time I like! I throw a pen. RAH! RAH! I pick the pen up again . . . they cannot contain the ANGROSAURUS REX girl, NO CHANCE!

I jump on my bed and roar and run about and throw a pillow and be the Angrosaurus rex girl child that I truly know I am. I feel big claws growing out of my fingertips, sharp and spiky and scary that could tear up any ice-cream van. My skin becomes all SO leathery, like a basketball and rippled and lizardy – like a dinosaur's! My eyes are neon sunshine yellow and piercing, with flickering dancing flames swishing about inside the pupils. My nostrils are huge! You could fit a rolling pin in them! My mouth roars open, I have hundreds and gazillions of mighty sharp pointy teeth like little glinting mountain knives that would burst an anything! And my tongue is purple and jagged and split like a ribbon and could karate-chop any person in a swish! My tail is long and fierce and strong, I am the ANGROSAURUS REX, NOT TO BE MESSED WITH! I AM THE FURIOUS ANGER-CHILD OF THE ACTUAL DEEP! This is my prison, my cell, my four walls! But you cannot keep this Angrosaurus locked away for ever . . .

RUUUUUUUOOOOOOOOORRRRRRRR!!!!!
ROOOOOOYYUUUUUUAAAAARRRRR!!!!

I stand with my legs apart, my feet planted into the ground, I squat down, close my eyes like I'm about to do a massive fart, ready to do the greatest roar of all time . . . RO—

'Darcy!' Mum shouts.

'Yeah?'

'SHUT UP!'

I peel open my writing book. It is possible to use this anger in a silent way . . .

Chapter Eleven

ANGROSAURUS REX HEADS OUT FOR A SNACK

WUUUUUUUUUUUOOOOOOOOORRRRRRR!!!!!!!

The Angrosaurus rex could just NOT help herself. She had to just nip into the town and EAT some people. It just had to be done.

RUUUUUUUUUUUOOOOOOARRRRRRI

WHAT ARE YOU DOING, ANGROSAURUS REX?

OH, JUST SIMPLY WAITING FOR THE BUS TO TOWN.

WHAT YOU GONNA DO WHEN YOU GET THERE?

HMM. MIGHT GO CINEMA. LOOK ROUND THE SHOPS AND PROBS EAT A FEW PEOPLE.

COOL.

And she did just that. BAM. In the town. The Angrosaurus rex roars down the high street, breaking brick houses, snapping trees, bending cars, ripping up bushes and shrubbery, bashing down roofs, eating clouds like candyfloss, forking the roads up like spaghetti on a fork. OH, SHE IS ANGRY.

'I AM SO ANGRY!'

She just eats a few people to whet her appetite. Chew. Chew. Bones. Crunch. Crunch. Crunch. Windows smash. Police sirens sing. Birds screech. The Angrosaurus rex roars mightily and ferociously.

'I WILL DESTROY YOU ALL! BUT FIRST I NEED TO EAT THIS RIGHT ANNOYING LITTLE BRAT BRUTE EVIL CHILD CALLED POPPY BURDOCK! OOOO, WHEN I GET HER, I WILL CHEW HER UP AND GULP HER HORRID LITTLE MENACING BODY DOWN WITH ONE SWALLOW!'

BANG. BASH. BOOM. BANG. BASH. BOOM. BANG. BASH. BOOM!

Then I just draw a bajillion scribbles. I lean my pen into the paper so hard that it leaves more

traces of every word for more and more pages underneath each one. My jaw is clenched, my body tense, my knuckles white, my eyes slit, my brows frown as I . . .

GRRRRRRRRRRRRRRRRRRRRRRRRRRRRRRIIII

ROOOOOOOOOOOOOOOAAAAAAAAARRRIIII

I feel a bit better now that I've letted off some steam. A bit. I close my book. Lie on my bed. This non-drama business is proving to be a lot LOT harder than I had anticipated, to be frank.

This is why I'm so glad I have my writing. I might get my spellings all wrong. My grammar all badly. My ideas might be jumbled and make no sense to anybody, but at least I have a place I can always go, in my head, on a page where I can be myself. Free and brave to do exactly what I want to do. And for that, I feel very lucky.

Chapter Twelve

Now that the truth is out I've decided to not bother wasting my time making advances towards Mum for her affection when she quite clearly couldn't care less or not if I got bulldozed down by a rhinoceros.

There's always my main man. *Dad*.

'You all right, Dad?' I say, so *sweetie kind*, when he comes back home from work.

'I'm fine, thank you, Darcy. How are you? I heard you guys got into a spot of trouble today?'

'Dad, it really isn't a biggie. Best not to make a thing out of a mountain.'

'Yes, best to forget it, I've already begun making the new wardrobe. Your mum's blaming me for that wardrobe, saying I built it wonky. I didn't think it was *that* wonky, did you?'

'No, Daddy.' I rub his arms. 'Not at ALL wonky. You are the most best carpenter in the world.'

'Why are you being so creepy?'

'I'm not. Do you want an ice-cold beer?'

'I won't say no.'

I know how to pour Dad's beer so good. He taught me. I don't mind teaching you. You have to just take a glass and hold it at an angle but not too much, and you just pour the beer in at the side and then start to tilt the glass up at the same time as pouring. It's quite hard because you have to do a pour AND a tilt at the same time. It's quite a lot like when you pat your head and rub your tummy. There should be a white frothy head on the beer at the end. That's what gives grown-ups those moustaches when they drink them. Once my mum shouted at a man in the pub because he told her that beers were just for men. And so my mum purposely drank a LOT of beers that night.

I get Dad a packet of crisps too from the treat cupboard. And a pack for me too. Obvs. Smoky bacon. Or salt and vin—

'What you do?' Hector asks.

'Taking care of my one parent,' I say.

'Can I have some crisps?'

'No, not before dinner.'

'You're having some.'

'I've said more words than you today, my tongue is tired.'

Hector begins to cry.

'Oh, don't cry.'

'You're having crisps and I not.'

'Have them then, THERE!' I throw a packet at him. 'Eat them quietly, suck the flavour off first, don't crunch or that mum of YOURS will tell you all off. Foot-rub, Dad?'

'No thanks, Darcy.'

'Massage, Dad?'

'You're all right. I've got a beer out here in the garden with my book. I'm just lovely.'

'Want me to do a tap dance? Some stand-up comedy? A magic show?'

'No! No!' he refuses, almost a little too quickly for my liking. 'But thank you.'

I watch Dad. His eyes are closed. The last of the sun on his face. I pick a lavender and I leave it by his hand as a gift. It seems a good time to ask the question I've been wanting to ask him.

'Dad. Am I your favourite?'

'Whatever you want,' he mumbles.

'Well, obviously, I'm your first born and that.'

'Yep.'

'So . . . what we saying, then? That a yes? I *am* your favourite, or . . .'

'If you want.'

'If I want or . . .'

'Darcy, I'm trying to relax, can't you see? I've been at work all day.'

'I just want you to say, DARCY, YOU ARE MY FAVOURITE.'

'Well, I'm not going to say that right now, no, because you are not my favourite, you're doing my head in.'

'FINE!' I huff loud and trot into the house. Lamb-Beth looks at me like perhaps I'm MAD. BUT I AM MAD. I am terribly unloved and so deprived of joy and activities, in this maze where the days never end, all spiralling into one of everlasting boredom drowning in my brain. I am ready to BLOW my steaming angro head off with rage and I'll start by slamming the door extra hard and giving this Burdock fam a TRUE BITTER PIECE OF MY ACTUAL MIND . . . open the door and SLLLLLLLLLLLAAAAA————

'Darcy!' Mum shouts. 'Dinner.'

YESSSSSSSSSSS! I sing a small 'excited for dinner' song.

And catch the door to stop it slamming. Just. In. Time.

Nice save, Darcy. Keep it cool. Don't let yourself down now, Darcy, you're halfway through the holidays, keep your enemies nice and close . . . don't be dramatic. Don't let that mum know you're on to her!

'What is it?'

'Pasta and red sauce.'

'Yum. And grated cheese?'

'And grated cheese, yes. You can grate some, and *this* time let's aim for grated cheese *without* your fingers in it.'

'That was ONCE!'

DON'T FALL FOR IT. Zip your lips! Keep calm. Anger boiling again. I WANT to throw this cheese grater up to the absolute moon and grate off its stupid big peery down face. Why does she always have to bring up old past-been news like that? OK, so there was some of my BODY in the cheese, but technically, unfortunately, I camed from MUM'S BODY so we have THE SAME BODY. SO why should it matter?

GGGGGRRRRR!

'Who wants a drink?' I whisper quietly as I get myself a glass of pink squash so I don't have to make anybody else one because it's long and all the glasses are broked or misty or in the dishwasher.

'Ask everybody please, Darcy, instead of just sorting yourself out.'

'I did!'

'You didn't.'

'I swear I did! But *anyway* . . . WHHHOOO WAAANNNTTS A DRIIIINNNKKK?'

'Me!'

'Ooh, me!'

'Please!'

'I'll have another beer please, thanks, Darcy.'

Great. Or course they do. Total. Eye. Ball. Roll.

Watching Mum eat pasta at dinner is just making me so cross. For no actual particular reason, to be honest, except the fact that she loves my younger sibling more than me. I start noticing how whenever Poppy makes a joke Mum just laughs that extra bit harderer. Or how Mum's nose scrinchies up so enchanted when she sees Poppy slurp up a worm of spaghetti like she's the cutest little button on the entire earth.

I try to be cute. Just for a second. Just as an experiment to see if she thinks I'm cute and enchanting too. I tangle up a big forkful of pasta and swivel it round into a pasta nest and then I slurp it up, making a huge kissing noise as I do it.

'Darcy! Stop it. Eat your food properly!' Mum immediately shouts.

'BUT I—'

Hold it down. Hold it down. Hold it.

'No buts, it's disgusting.'

DISGUSTING? *Disgusting?*

'But Poppy just did—'

No point even trying. It's as evident as the day is . . . I don't know what day it is as it's the summer holidays and all the days are rolling to one. *Whatever.*

I shake my head at Mum. I'm thinking . . . *I really tried with you, Mum.* I really tried. I know *exactly* when I'm not wanted. It's just me and Dad in this world. Me and my dad. In our wonderful drama-free lifestyle.

But then it occurs to me that that would be impossible. Here I am trying my absolute very best to not be dramatic when both my parents are the most dramatic parents ever even borned! They *made* me. And if the dominant ingredient in both their DNAs is drama . . . well, that's something that's surely gonna be passed down to me!

No wonder I'm so diseased with drama! I've got a double dose of it! The drama plague! I'm riddled!

I feel the urge to write about this. Explore this subject good and proper!

Chapter Thirteen

AN INHERITANCE OF DRAMA FOR THE LORD OF DRAMA

Casper was born in a volcano. Don't worry, it wasn't erupting at the time. But it could have been. These things are terribly temperamental.

You see, Casper's parents were wild thrill-seeking explorers and were always off tracking strange creatures, learning circus tricks in the wild or seeing the stars in their rocket ship. And while they saw the world, Casper would be babysat by the old lady next door who they called Crowe. Because she was one – an old one too. Here, in the cosy clutch of her

221

wallpapered living room, he would draw crazy
illustrations with his crayons of all the places he
expected his parents to be.

But he never expected them to
go up in their rocket ship and never
come back down again . . . .

I know. It's a VERY sad
start to a story. But immediately
the old babysitter, Crowe, took
Casper under her wing. Crowe was
the opposite to Casper's parents and
was pretty quiet and simple. She would eat soup
and drippy bread and talk to her cat. But Casper
loved her because although Crowe's house was
pretty boring, yes, and the heating was *always* on
FULL BLAST, explorer she was not. And that
suited Casper, he didn't want any drama in his
life at all. He wanted to just be a normal quiet
boy.

But one day, when Crowe was popping out
to pay her newspaper bill at the newsagent's,

she was scooped up by a dustbin truck. Chewed to pieces in the metal industrial jaw of the thing. She *was* wearing her shiny pea-green anorak which definitely could have been mistaken for a bin liner. And that was that. She was gone. What a *rubbish* way to die. Ha. (Sorry, couldn't resist!)

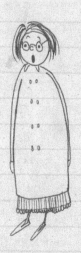

And when Casper heard the news, he was very sad. He didn't have anybody else left to love and nobody to love him back either. He crawled up into a round ball and wrapped the duvet over his head. The house felt silent and bigger than usual. The familiar rhythms of living with another human. They were all gone. He felt his little heart freeze and turn to stone.

The cat jumped up onto his bed to sleep.

It was reassuring to have a beating heart on his.
The warmth of a quiet friend in the darkness.

Puuuuuuurrr. Purrrrrr. Purrrrrr.

The cat dozed and together they fell asleep.

But Casper was woken up first thing. To a
terrible retching sound. His body arched all tight
and rounded, his eyes popping out, his black
coarse hairs on end, his ears pinned back. The
cat was choking! Gagging! *Oh no! No!* Not the
cat too!

And then the cat was sick.

Gross. Casper had to get up and clear up the
sick . . . wait . . . was that a note? Inside the
drooling, curdling, lumpy, pale, cakey, clumpy cat
sick?

No? But that did look like writing. He didn't want to touch the cat sick. *Eugh. Shudder.* But there was a tiny part of Casper that couldn't help himself. He gently fingered through the sick and pulled out the little scrap of paper.

Casper felt slightly crazy as he unravelled the note but he did it all the same, unfolding the words carefully to read:

If you are reading this it means I am dead.

Sorry about that. It wouldn't have been my fault.

I know I was old and boring, but listen, my house is not quite as granny as it always seemed. Even the most boring people can have a little trick up their sleeve.

Your parents left you something when they went, you inherited something very special . . .

I think you are ready for it.

To receive it go to my en-suite bathroom and you'll know what to do next.

Love and kisses to my cat,

Your neighbour, Crowe . . .

P.S. And remember, do not fight who you really are.

Casper felt as though he'd been struck by lightning. Remember, he HATED drama. He didn't want anything unusual. He didn't want an 'inheritance'. He wanted to just carry on as normal in Crowe's house doing all the things Crowe would do like drink tea and talk to the cat. But curiosity was already tingling in his fingertips . . .

Casper, without thinking, ran into Crowe's bedroom, and immediately her en-suite bathroom door creaked open. He closed his eyes shut for fear of the surprise . . . but nothing.

Casper almost felt disappointed — he'd expected something tremendous . . .

Just in case, Casper snooped about the cupboards: just bottles and toothpaste and creams. Casper, nosily, looked into the taps, the

shower, the bath. *No, nothing strange.* He lifted
the toilet lid. And at the bottom of the toilet,
deep in the bowl, written in curly gold ink, were
the words:

FLUSH ME.

Casper had never taken instructions from a
toilet before, but the flame of curiosity inside him
had been lit. The flush was a pull chain that
hung from the top of the toilet pipe. A long metal
rope with a wooden handle
on the end. 'Here
goes . . .' Casper closed
his eyes and yanked the
chain of the toilet, and
before he knew it
he shot up
through the roof.

So much for
no drama.

Casper's head
popped out of a

stone well. *Where was he?* He could see a
gravel drive and fields and fields in all shades
of green behind him — and in front of him was
the most fantastically grand, huge mansion.
Looking back down, the inside of the well was
wet, cold and damp; slimy with grass and weeds,
whereas he was completely untouched. It didn't
seem likely that he'd crawled through it.

A shiny black crow flew down towards him.
Her eyes were black and beady like beetles. He
knew it was strange, but the crow felt awfully
familiar, but he couldn't tell why. Her eyes were
almost like Crowe's . . . and then
she began to speak. Casper
was shocked. A talking crow?
But he listened . . .

'And here you are, Casper, you
brave young thing . . . would you
like to know what you've inherited?' Her voice
was identical to Crowe's voice but it seemed
somehow younger, lighter and more free.

'Err . . . I guess so . . .'

'Your parents asked me to take care of their drama until you were old enough to have it yourself, but now that I am gone too, I think it's for the best that it is yours . . . my dear boy, you've inherited drama!'

'Drama?' Casper shook his head in fear. 'I don't think I want any drama. My parents were crazy explorers – I don't think I want that!'

The crow began again. 'There is a beautiful, big world out there, Casper. It is up to you to explore it. All is not as it seems – let me show you how to start your adventure.' And the crow dropped a gold key into Casper's palm and flapped away into the wind.

'Wait! Come back!' Casper cried . . . but it was too late. She was gone.

The key burned into his trembling palm. It was tingling.

The mansion stood there. Tall. Welcoming . . . exciting.

He had a key. Surely, you're not *breaking in* if you have a key?

And Casper slid the gold key into the lock. It groaned open as though it belonged to him and he stepped inside. The mansion was like a castle; a big stone floor and plants like palm trees. Stained-glass windows and huge ornaments and antiques. It was opulent and decadent. So regal, like the house of a king.

'Welcome home, Mr Casper,' said the butler. 'Did you have a nice day exploring? May I take your coat?'

'Excuse me?'

'The chef has your favourite, *rightly exactly cooked oven chips without burning, baked beans and grated melted cheese,* with a glass of lemonade and chocolate ice cream for after with cookies crumbled on top, waiting for you in the dining room at one o'clock.'

'The chef? The dining room?' Casper rubbed his eyes wearily. *How did they know his favourite food? How did he land in this spooky dream?* 'How will I know when it's one o'clock?'

'Forgotten already about your genius clock! Silly billy!' The butler looked up to the sky, and as if on cue a glass bottle filled with water smashed to the ground.

'What is that?'

'That's your clock invention: you said that every second a drop of water would fill the bottle, every minute the bottle – heavier with water – would tilt, until on the hour the bottle completely capsizes from its balance in the bracket and comes crashing to the floor.'

A maid in rubber shoes came out and dusted away the glass, wiped up the water and pattered away as though she had never existed.

'Seems like a *lot* of trouble to go to just to tell the time.'

'Don't be ridiculous, sir, it is rather over the top. And dramatic . . .' The butler politely smiled. 'But that's how you like it, that's you all over, the Lord of Drama!'

'The Lord of–?'

And then suddenly, one by one, heads popped out from the mansion, behind walls, down stairs, out from behind the clock. There were servants, chefs, tigers, clowns, jesters, a spaceman, a mermaid . . . all shouting the word, 'Drama!'

Before Casper knew it, he was a V.I.P. front-row guest of a musical dedicated to him. An all-singing, all-dancing performance about 'Casper, the Lord of Drama'.

Which was a song, all about, well . . . how much Casper loved drama.

'No, no . . .' Casper shook his head. 'No, I need to get back home.'

'This *is* your home,' the butler offered kindly.

'Where's the cat?'

'Here, sir.'

And out from underneath a chair, the cat snaked happily. This boggled Casper's mind even further. Had he really shot up a toilet into this crazy mansion?

'Come and eat, sir, and then get some rest. You must be awfully tired.'

Casper tossed and turned in his giant, wobbling waterbed. He had just been 'acted' out

a bedtime story and was feeling more awake
than he had done EVER. He was never going
to get to sleep in this mad house. Not with the
singing and dancing and acrobatics and tigers
roaring and mermaids splashing and giants roaming
and the stupid glass-bottle clock smashing every
hour.

Still, eventually, sleep came upon him. He felt
webbed in jelly, like he was nestled in a big
spoonful of gluey sweet medicine.

And then suddenly off went the sirens. The
whole entire mansion was alive with red, blue,
white lights.

Casper sat bolt upright in his bed. Panicked
with fear. His eyes bulging with terror as the shrill
of the sirens fizzed through his ears. His heart
was thumping. What was happening? *Was there a
fire?*

'EMERGENCY, EMERGENCY!' boomed a
scratchy, scary computer robot voice.
'EMERGENCY!'

Casper screamed, 'AARGH! HELP! WHAT EMERGENCY?'

'EMERGENCY!' the speaker repeated.

Suddenly a herd of fuzzy, furry, multi-coloured hairy bodies bounced into Casper's bedroom. Casper screamed again, his throat

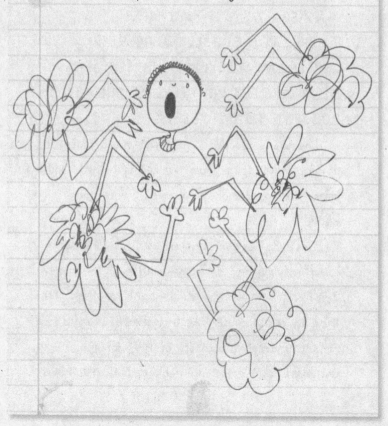

ripping with fear. They were like man-sized
pom-pom sea urchins, without eyes or mouths or
ears, only long arms with big chubby, fluffy
fingers!

'AARGGGGGHHH! GET OUT! GET OUT!'
Casper screamed.

'EMERGENCY!' repeated the voice.
'EMERGENCY! SUBJECT HAS BEEN
AVOIDING TICKLES! SUBJECT HAS
BEEN AVOIDING TICKLES! SUBMIT
SUBJECT TO TICKLES!'

The sirens stopped and disco music came on,
a mirror ball down from the ceiling turned, spitting
mirror starry diamonds all over the bedroom
walls.

'Tickles? Tickles?' Casper was so confused.
'What's going on? It's the middle of the night! I
don't want to be tickled! I want to sleep!' He
tried to crawl under the bed sheets, burying
himself under the blankets of his wobbly
waterbed as the big multi-coloured fluffy things

236

and their long arms tickled Casper all over. He screamed and fought them off but couldn't help it. He was laughing his head off. The tickling was too much. His ribs ached. His belly tightened, his face squeezed up, clenched into a tight smile. His eyes watered and the furry, faceless things just kept tickling and tickling until Casper was red in the face and could no longer breathe.

The disco music stopped and the fluffy things stopped tickling and left the room.

'EMERGENCY RECTIFIED. SERVICE RESUMED. THANK YOU FOR YOUR CO-OPERATION.'

How dare those monster things just burst into his room like that!

GRRRRRRRRRRRR! *Where was that stupid butler? He needed a word with him this minute. If this really was his house there needed to be some new house rules.*

He found the butler bouncing on a trampoline by the stairs in a ball gown.

'Good morning/night, Lord of Drama. Is everything OK?' The butler took a break from bouncing to wipe sweat from his brow.

'What are you doing?'

'Rehearsing.'

'Rehearsing for what?'

'Your breakfast show of the Bouncing Princess. I play the princess. She bounces.'

'I don't want a breakfast show.'

'You don't want a breakfast show? But you're the Lord of Drama! You're having spicy eggs and a Cappuccino with an Attitude Problem to go with it.'

'No! I don't want spicy eggs and a Cappuccino with an Attitude Problem to go with it either! I just want *normal*.' Casper shook his head. 'I don't want all this drama.'

'But Lord of Drama-'

'STOP CALLING ME THE LORD OF DRAMA!' Casper roared.

'Well, don't be so dramatic then and we can think of a new title for you.'

Casper could see his point.

'My parents were the dramatic ones. They loved drama. They chased it. And it's what killed them. I don't want that. I want simplicity.'

'You want to be the Lord of Boring?'

'Well . . . no . . . not really, but fine, yes, if that's what I have to be to get a normal life . . . then fine. I'll be the Lord of Boring.'

Oh, but that was worse. MUCH worse.

'Cardboard soup,' moaned the butler, 'with grey tea.'

'Cardboard soup?'

'Yes, that's right, Lord of Boring. Followed by the news in the drawing room with more newspapers and an afternoon session of watching paint dry.'

'Paint dry? I don't want to watch paint dry.'

The butler was now staring blankly into space.

'I don't want to be the Lord of Boring,' Casper declared. 'It's just as extreme, just boring too. It's just as dramatic. Do I still have to be a Lord? Can't I JUST be a normal person . . . Is there no middle ground? No balance?'

'But you are born with drama, your parents are dramatic and so are you. So what will it be? Boring . . . or dramatic?' the butler asked.

Casper was already feeling the horrid cardboard soup repeating on him. 'I guess it will have to be dramatic.'

And at that moment a rocket ship burst
through the ceiling of the mansion. The stone floor
smashed to pieces, the glass windows cracked.
The butler shielded himself behind a quivering
plant. The rocket was alive, roaring, hissing, yellow
fire burning bright. Split shards of metal and the
burnt smell of petrol. Puffs of black smoke plumed
through the air.

The beaten-up metal door of the rocket ship
swung open. 'WOOOOO-HOOOOO! That was
FUN!' It was Casper's mum, giggling as she
high-fived Casper's dad. They peeled off their
helmets.

'See, I told you that your mum would like a
motorbike!' Dad chuckled to Casper.

'We missed you, Casper! Were you well behaved on our week away?'

'Week away? You've been gone for ages. I thought you were never coming back!'

'Never coming back?'

'You went in a rocket ship!'

'Casper, we went away for a week on Dad's new motorbike!'

'You left me with a stranger!'

'You mean Mrs Crowe? She's an old friend of mine.'

'She got eaten by a dustbin.'

'That imagination of yours is out of control. Casper, you are the most dramatic person in the entire world.'

Casper looked down at the table in front of him and saw a drawing pad where he had drawn the most elaborate drawings. Of a mansion, of a rocket ship, of an old lady being eaten by a dustbin truck, of tickle monsters and cardboard soup.

Casper's mum admired the drawings and patted her son on the head. 'I don't know where you get it from.' She winked as she walked away, leaving little Casper in her shadow.

Chapter Fourteen

Me and my *best friend*, Dad, have been getting on like a house on fire; we pretty much put the 'bond' in bonding.

I've basically decided the next three weeks of these summer holidays is really gonna drag unless I find something to do. Like perhaps get myself invited to work with him or something. Something's *got* to give.

'Dad.'

'You're still doing that creepy voice again, Darcy.'

'I'm not.'

'You are, but anyway, what do you want?'

'Can I come to work with you one day?'

'Bored, are you?'

'No, not bored, just so interested in what the absolute king of my life does all day.'

'Well, put it this way, I'd MUCH rather be at home with you lot enjoying our lovely new house than at work.'

'Really?'

'Yes. You don't want to come to the workshop. It's cold. Sawdust gets all in your eyes.'

'I think I do want to come.'

'I'll think about it.'

'Why can't you just think about it now?'

'I need to talk to my colleagues.'

'But you're the boss.'

'Sort of. John is the main boss.'

'No he's not. Mum told me already that you're the one that does all the work and John Pincher just gets all the money.'

'Oh, did she now?' Dad laughs.

'Mum says he's hardly ever even there, and even when he does come in he's just a nuisance and gets in everybody's way because he doesn't know what he's doing.'

'And what makes you think a gobby little girl barging about the place won't get in anybody's way?'

'I loved it last time.'

'That was a quick visit, not all day.'

'Oh, Dad, *please*?'

Dad goes back to his paper. Lamb-Beth, my beauty lamb, is flopped across his lap, sleeping so wonderfully cutely.

'It's not fair on Hector and Poppy if I just take you.'

'Take them another day.'

'I can't, monkey, it's not safe! I work around lots of machinery – look how many scraps I get myself into.' He holds his hands up. They are covered in tiny bloody nips.

'Dad, you get splinters. I think I can handle a splinter.'

Dad looks at me, trying to work me out as

though he is some knight here to judge if I am ready to join his round table or something.

'OK. OK. You can come.'

'Really?'

'Yes. Really. But don't get too excited. It really isn't that fun.'

'Can I bring Lamb-Beth?'

'Don't push it.'

Oh, sick. Will is going to go absolutely mental when I tell him when he gets home. That I did a day's actual GRAFT! Like a builder person! Absolutely brilliant. This is going to be the best day of my entire life.

'Errr. What are you doing?' Poppy catches me in the kitchen leaning over the breadboard.

'Making sandwiches.'

'That looks like a packed lunch to me.'

'Well, so what if it is?'

'Who is it a packed lunch for?'

'Me.'

She comes over and spies my creations. Cheese, pickle, salad.

'They are **DAD** flavours!' She glares. 'Where you going?'

'To work.'

'With who?'

'None of your beeswax.'

'**NOT WITH DAD?**'

'I'm not saying I am but I'm not saying I'm not.'

'Oh, my actual days, no you are **NOT**!'

'Oh yes I am.'

'No!'

'Yes!'

'No!'

'Yes!'

'But we aren't allowed in Dad's workshop because he says it's dangerous, all saws and stuff.'

'Well, I'm old enough now, Poppy. I know that's not really that nice for you to hear but I've waited my time; a couple more years to go and maybe you'll be able to come to be making visits to Dad's work too.'

'I can't believe this.'

'Believe it, Poppy. It's very, very real.'

'Why would Dad be taking YOU and not me?'

'Who knows?' I dab a crumb of cheese off the side and pop it in my mouth. 'Maybe . . . I'm just Dad's favourite?'

HA! Suck on THAT sweetie of own medicine, Poppy Burdock!

But the smile is quite swiftly wiped from my actual face because Poppy screams her spoiled head off and cries her stupid sorry eyes out.

Cut to me and my best friend, Dad, AND tagalong Poppy, leaving the house for a day at Dad's work.

'Shotgun front seat!' I push Poppy out of the way.

'It's my turn.'

'I think we all know that you have scraped your way on to this trip. Now get in the back.'

I've worn overalls. OK. They are denim and they also might be dungarees that are slightly (OK, a LOT) a bit tight and is making my fat bulge a bit around my arms, but they look fine, with a bright yellow T-shirt underneath and Dr Martens lace-up boots.

'You look like a minion,' Poppy smirks.

'I look *practical*, actually, and as though I make stuff out of wood.'

'You can't even walk in them. Look. They are so tight. Like you're going to burst out of the seams. You've had those dungarees since you were my age.' What a toad!

'They are OVERALLS!'

'Whatevs.'

I put the carrier bag of lunch down by my feet. It's bulging full of delicious snacks and sandwiches prepared by me. Even though all the sandwiches had to go in an old bread bag because we never have clingfilm or foil or sandwich boxes at ours. We just aren't that organized family.

Dad takes us to the CAFE first. It looks like the word café but you have to say it like this – 'CAFF' – otherwise people laugh at you. Cafés are luxurious posh places with croissants and hummus and frothy coffee that let babies and prams in and do pesto on toasted paninis. CAFFs are full of bacon sandwiches and coffee made from powder with cheap plastic seats that are joineded to the table.

'Right, what do you girls want?'

'There's too many choices of the same thing, just in different orders.'

'OK, have a think.' Dad walks up to the man behind the counter. 'I'll get a Full English breakfast please.'

'Me too,' Poppy quickly blurts.

SO ANNOYING. It's meant to be me and Dad getting the same thing. Why does she have to get all involved and copy? I can't have the same as her now or else it will look as though I've copied her and like I don't have a regular at the local CAFF, which I absolutely must have if me and Dad are going to continue this routine. I feel pressure. I can't be dramatic. I just have to hold it down and restrain myself like a composed ballet dancer or a chick in a kimono. Dad's got his money in his hand waiting to pay, the man behind the till is smiling, his pen anxiously hovering, waiting to write my order down. All right, all right . . .

'Summer holidays, is it?' He smiles at my dad; he has a gold tooth.

'Yes.' Dad grins. 'It's *take your girls to work day* apparently.'

'Hah! I always have my lot in here! They eat me out of the business. Course, they're all on holiday right now!'

JEALOUS! I wish Will was back from his. He'd

know just what to order at the CAFF.

I still can't choose.

'Sure you are gonna be able to handle a Full English breakfast?' the man asks Poppy.

'Yes, I think I will do actually,' Poppy snaps back like a smartypants and the man laughs.

'Ha-ha! Cheeky one here!'

Oh, SHOVE OFF, Poppy.

'Come on, Darcy, what would you like?'

'I'll get some beans . . . in a bowl . . . please.'

'With . . . toast?'

No. That's so boring. I can't get toast. Toast is for

normal days. Not days like today that are exciting and in CAFFs.

'With . . .' My eyes scatter across the words of greasy gloopy ingredients before they settle on 'garlic bread'.

Dad looks at me funny. 'Sure that's all you want, D?'

'I'm sure,' I say, but the word is not sure at all.

The CAFF man laughs. 'So two Full English and a bowl of beans with a side of garlic bread.'

I must have missed the all-important memo that told us that Full English breakfast came with chips. CHIPS. Actually allowed to be having chips at breakfast. I want to cry when Dad and Poppy's mound of food comes. All brown juicy plump sausages and slobbery fatty bacon. Beans spilling everywhere and sunshine eggs, all shiny and white with glossy yellow mirrors in the middle. Hash browns look all crispy and yum and there's toast too. Heaps of buttered triangles and a piece of fried too. And mountains of hot chips.

'And the beans and garlic bread.'

Which comes exactly as it reads. A bowl of soupy beans with a layer of bean skin across the top, and four horse-ear-shaped slices of obviously once frozen garlic bread, for dipping, I guess.

DE-PRESS-ING. I feel my hands stick to the sticky, grease-slicken table.

'OOooo!' Poppy says, being all so showy-offy. 'Look at all this.'

'Lubbly jubbly!' Dad says, sipping his tea, rubbing his hands together nicely. 'Don't tell Mum I come here, will you? It's just a special occasion, cos I got my girls with me.'

Even though we are pretty sure Dad comes here every day!

'We won't tell!' Poppy shrieks, and she squirts red sauce everywhere.

Oh, she is so disloyal. What a backstabbing little fox. She won't tell Mum! HA! NOW whose side is she on? Unbelievable.

I dip my garlic bread into my beans, scooping it up like some kind of green-flecked shovel of grease. I look about the caff walls. Builders' bums creak out of loose worn jeans. Grubby nails eat bacon sandwiches and slurp strong tea from polystyrene cups. Don't they wash their hands in these places? I think people might be a bit laughing at me in the caff. But I think it's my outfit. It hurts to sit down. My tummy is all squeezed in tight. I feel sick. I do look like a minion. A try-hard builder. And under the bright neon fluorescent lights I look ever more worserer. My T-shirt is a hideous acid banana yellow. A try-hard, alien, minion builder. Eating garlic bread and beans.

We get to Dad's workshop. He's got these other

people that work for him. They are not all here today but we know most of them. The radio plays, and because it's a nice day the shutter is up and sunshine streams in. The light breeze takes turns in scooping up curls of discarded wood; they look like blossom petals. The air smells thick and sandy. The concrete floor is a bed for a hamster. Sawdusty. Like a planet of grated parmesan cheese snow.

'UH-OH! HERE COMES TROUBLE!' John Pincher breathes all over us with his coffee breath of mud. 'I can never get Donald down here! I keep telling him it would be fun, but oh no!'

'We went to the café and had breakfast,' Poppy tells him.

'That place is in my bad books!' John frowns. 'Look what they've done to me!' He gives his fat belly a poke and laughs. 'Right, best be back to work then.'

Dad rolls his eyes at us because we know just as much as Dad does that John Pincher doesn't know WHAT he's doing.

Dad gives us each a pair of goggles to wear so we don't get sawdust in our eyes.

The equipment looks awfully exciting, if you ask me. Big shiny teeth of saws glint at us, drills and other machinery that looks like it could kill you if you wanted it to. The radio is there too, singing pop songs.

'Dad, can we make a doll's house?' Poppy suggests.

'It takes a long time to make a doll's house,' Dad says.

'Can we make a . . .' I can't think of anything . . .

All my brain is shouting is STICK, STICK, STICK . . . Who wants to make a stick?

'Can we make a puzzle?' Poppy asks.

'Yeah, we can make a puzzle.' He smiles. Damn Poppy and all her wood toys that she can immediately think of. 'Why don't you sit up here and use some paper to draw out what your puzzle is going to look like?'

We sit with pencils and tracing paper. I feel sick. My dungarees are bursting me in all shut. *Bleugh.*

'Hey, sweeties, long time no see!' It's Madison. We LOVE Madison. She has long dyed plaits and a pierced nose and drinks ginger tea. And she is so good at cutting and chopping wood and making any magical design you want. My dad says that Madison is the most creative wizard girl he knows and can turn any lump of old wood into anything. A desk. A rocking chair. A lamp. And even though Madison works with wood all day she has the softest, most gentle hands that wouldn't even bruise a peach. Her fingers, made just entirely for carving, are light and lovely. Her voice is all croaky and lush too and she hums when she makes things. Unfortunately she isn't wearing dungarees, which makes me think perhaps I got the dungaree/overall look completely wrong.

'Is it true you have a pet hippo?' I ask Madison.

'Ha, did your dad tell you? Well, yes, back home in Tanzania, when I was small, we used to know a hippo – we named her Galaxy. And Galaxy would come chill on our front step. She used to eat yams and drink coffee!'

'Coffee!'

'Yup! Buckets of coffee and sacks of yam!'

'No way!'

'Yes way. You guys have a lamb, don't you?'

'Yep.'

'See, that's pretty cool.'

'I know.'

'What we doing here then, ladies?'

'Making puzzles.'

'Cool! Let me help you.'

We begin designing and drawing. Quietly listening to the music and Madison's soft hum of peaceful concentration. The beautiful silver rings on her fingers are mesmerizing as she works. I want to be here every day, so calm like this, working with Madison in the sunshine, making puzzles all day. Maybe one day I'll work my way up to not just building puzzles but park benches and stuff. Maybe Madison can be my best friend instead of Dad.

But then the worst thing happens.

It's definitely not my fault.

It's the tight minion try-hard builder dungaree overalls mixed with the garlic bread and all the beans being so incredibly squashed and pressed up all bulging against my tummy that did it.

I try to clench up and hold it in. But before I know it . . .

A terrible, terrible *SBD** fart sneaks out my bum.

* SBD = SILENT BUT DEADLY

261

I am literally using all my might to hope it doesn't smell. But you know, sometimes you just *know*?

Now, this is a moment when I really could not tell what exactly was going to happen. Was Poppy going to pretend to smell it or not? Chances were she might think the fart belonged to Madison and she certainly wouldn't want to embarrass her. But then again, if she suspected me then she might bait me up because she wouldn't want Madison to think the fart belonged to her!

I think Poppy will know the fart is mine anyway, as all farts have their own housy smell. When you know a person you can usually recognize their farts straight away, because you know what that person eats and drinks, plus you can smell the house inside their fart. Sucking up the smell and pumping out a more disgusting version of the same smell. It's like the farts replicate the familiar smell of a house and puff it out in pieces to always remind you of home. It's quite sweet really.

Maybe if I edge close enough to the door the smell will waft away with the warm summer breeze?

Maybe the harsh woody smell of sawdust will blend it away, masking it nicely?

Maybe . . . *oh no, they've just actually smelt it.*

Madison politely smiles and twitches her nose. If I wasn't the person who farted, or if I had but was watching her through a screen, I would never have even noticed she was breathing in a fart; she's *that* subtle.

But Poppy is not quite as forgiving.

'Bleugh, Darcy, Farty Mcfarty-son! What on earth was that?'

'What?'

'It smells like you ate a bin.'

'It wasn't me.'

'If it wasn't you, how did you know to say it *wasn't* you?'

'Whoever smelt it, dealt it.'

'As if – look, the wind is travelling this way.'

'Well, maybe it was John Pincher?'

John does have his bum crack on display as he's bent over, pretending to be sawing.

'The fart could have escaped out of the gap?'

'Hm. Yeah, maybe.'

Madison giggles.

We forget about the fart itself as the lingering smell dissolves. But I can't help but look at Poppy and think . . . *Do I HAVE to love you? I mean, I know you're my sister and everything, but you are SO annoying.*

I have the sweats. My stupid outfit is so tight. But I'm not going to make a deal out of that or anything. A good work person never blames their tools *or* their costume. So I won't either. I'm very professional, as you can probably tell.

'Eat our sandwiches in the sun, shall we?' Dad suggests at lunch time. I am quite greedy so can't not have a sandwich even though my whole body feels like an overstuffed teddy bear.

'Yay!' Poppy claps, elated. She can't be hungry either surely after eating her giant king-sized breakfast.

'I'm changing MY name to Madison,' says Poppy. 'When you get a new best friend it's very nice to take on their name.'

Oh, super. What am I meant to do now she's taken on Madison's name already. Take on my best friend Dad's name? Can you imagine me going about my life?

'Hi there, nice to meet you, what's your name?'

'Oh, you know, just *Dad.*'

John Pincher tells Dad that he's just going to *meet a client.* I think that's their roles: that John goes out and meets all the rich friends and Dad runs the workshop, making all the rich people's dreams come to life with wood.

We eat on a patch of grass by Dad's workshop. Dad has a little pencil behind his ear and all grub on his fingers. It makes me quite proud to see him enjoying my sandwiches.

'Wow, this is a treat, having a nice lunch made for me.' He smiles. 'Cheers, Darcy.'

There are crisps and chocolate and fruit for afters. It would've been a mucher more better picnic if I had longer in advance to prepare. I could've like gone to the fish-and-chip shop the night before and wrapped

them up in birthday-present paper. I suppose the chips would be cold, but who cares, it's chips.

There's this such annoying wasp hanging around pestering me to the absolute most. I just hate wasps – what is the point of them?

'WHAT IS THE POINT OF YOU?' I scream at the wasp, but it's too rude to listen. It's dangling all around the sandwiches and won't leave us alone. I'm getting all hot and flustered and sweaty because I feel the pressure a bit – this is a lunch I had prepared, so I want Dad to enjoy it because then he might bring me to work more often and Madison and I can be more closer friends – if she manages to forget about my fart – and I can say to Dad that I'll make his lunch every day and maybe give up school for good because perhaps he will see something in me and I can just be his number-one true real-life apprentice instead of doing this school business any more and we can change the workshop name to *Burdock and Daughter* and it will be great. But for now . . . I feel sick. The sun on my face and back. *Beat. Beat. Beat.* The buzzy hissy wasp. *Buzz. Hiss. Buzz.* The food all trapped. Like I'm a pregnant whale. All stuffed up and beginning to creep up my neck in my throat pipe because there is no more space for any food anyWHERE.

I put my hand down on the sandwiches to cover over the paper and – BAM! – the wasp stings me.

'AARGH!'

'Darcy, what?'

'The wasp, it—'

And then I'm sick.

BLLLLLLLLLLEEEEEUUUUGGGGGGHHH!

'Oh!'

'Get a glass of water, Poppy . . . and ask Madison for a towel,' Dad says in panic. 'And something for the sting, a first-aid kit or something . . . Darcy, D, you OK, monkey?'

'Aarghhhhhhh, I was sick, I hate being sick.'

'Don't cry, I know you do, don't cry.'

And tears are all running out my eyes and I'm just so upsetted because I was looking SO majorly forward to this day for my whole entire, well . . . yesterday night . . . and now it's ruined because my hand is throb-a-bob-bobbing, all red and stingy, and the sick is all tasting disgusting and coming out my nose is all little round bullet-shaped naked beans without any sauce. My throat is so sore and itchy and my tummy hurts. Still my ribs are all jammed and tight and my mouth all gooey and watery. And it's still so hot and I can't breathe at all really that good, and then I bursted into big more tears. And meaning still not to be dramatic but can't help it.

'I know, I know, darling, it's not nice to be sick, is it? Shall we get you out of these dungarees, they look a bit tight?'

'They aren't dungarees,' I sob. 'Dad, they're overalls.'

'Overalls. Sorry. I meant to say overalls. They look very nice.'

'No they don't. They look ugly.'

'No they don't. Look, I have a spare T-shirt upstairs. It will be cool, like a big oversized dress. Shall we change you into that?'

I nod.

'OK, come on then, sweetheart.'

My belly flobbers out with a wobbling, almost euphoric sense of RE-LIEF. It has red lines all over it from the press of the evil dungaree material. It feels amazing to have them off. Like a birthday or weeing when you're desperate or going to sleep when you're really tired or peeling your boiling hot socks off in the night and releasing the trapped feet.

I am R-E-A-D-Y for work! All I need is for Dad to teach me how to use this saw and that old drill and this useful power-tool sander thing and I'll be making garden sheds in no time!

'I think we should go home, girls.'

'What?'

'You're not well, doll, and Mum wants you to come home – she's worried you might have a virus.'

'A virus? No, Dad, I'm absolutely fine.' I shake my head. 'Look at me – I can twirl around and spin about and roly-poly and jump jack!'

Dad smiles. 'I know, monkey D, but we never know. We don't want you to get any worse.'

'I won't get any worse – look, it was only because my outfit was too small.'

'I told you,' Poppy remarks.

'Shut up you, Poppy.'

'Come on, girls, in the car,' says Dad.

And I can't even make a fuss. Or be sad. Or be angry because all those things count as being dramatic. I can't be sick in the school holidays, that really is a liberty. Everyone knows you're only meant to be sick on an actual school day so you get a day off. A.N.N.O.Y.I.N.G.

Mum is such an expert at ruining my fun. Could she make it ANY more clearer that I am not her best daughter? How does she manage to ruin my life even from afar?

Livid.

I rehearse my normal straight face in the car on the way home. Poppy is so fuming at me because she wasn't ill or anything and has to come home when she obviously wanted it to just be her and Madison all day, probably wearing BFF necklaces. My wasp sting still pounds and pangs in my hand but I just have to get over that. I JUST hate wasps. Stupid useless things. At least bees make honey and die once they sting you up. What good does a wasp do?

Nish.

I charge into the house and ignore Mum.

'Darcy, are you OK?'

'Yes. I'm fine.'

And I shoot up the stairs to my room.

Moments later and the old witch is back. 'Sweetie, I've run you a nice hot bath.'

'Why?'

'Because you're sick. Thought it would be nice to get you cleaned up.'

She is right. I stink like a baby's nappy.

'And I want to have a look at your sting too.'

Why is she even bothering? Pretending to care?

The sucking-up doesn't really stop there either. It's warm fluffy towels and a scented candle. It's one of her bestest unopened packets of stolen hotel slippers, fresh and ready for me to wear for when I get out. Then

she's made me hot tea and a piece of toast and leaves me on the couch all cosied up like a newborn mouse wrapped in felt. Little snoozy Lamb-Beth is curled around my shoulders like a scarf. She dumps the remote control for the TV in my lap and suggests me watching a film while she creams my sting.

Poppy looks at me from the couch, her face upturned and completely crinkled up in jealous disgust. *Oh, sorry about me, Poppy, getting the A-star treatment.*

Who's the *best* one now then, eh?

'Mum?' I ask in a tiny quiet voice. 'You remember

when we broke the wardrobe and Donald ripped your skirt?'

'Err . . . yes . . . how could I ever forget?'

'You heard a bang and you shouted Poppy's name and not mines or Hector's – is that because she's your favourite one?'

'What are you on about?' She laughs. 'Is that what *this* is all about?' She tuts, kissing my head. 'Silly billy-goat, no.' She laughs some more. 'I shouted Poppy's name because she is the one that usually does something naughty.'

'Oh.' Oh. 'So basically you were telling her off before you'd even seen what happened?'

'Basically, yes,' she whispers. 'I do not trust that little menace troublemaker one bit!' She laughs. 'But shhhh, don't tell her that.'

'OK, so who really is your favourite?'

'You don't have favourites, Darcy. It's impossible – you are all my babies and I love you all identical to the most anybody could love anything. Three peas in a pod.'

Chapter Fifteen

WEEK 4/6

It's a new day in the endless foreverness of the summer-holiday empty blissness. And thankfully I am feeling much better. The sun is shining and Lamb-Beth is playing very nicely, I must say so myself, in the garden. We have the radio on and Mum has given us a really nice job. It's a big drawer fulled up to the top with all the house wires and plugs and we have to untangle them all nicely and lay them out. We are not allowed to plug them into anything unless we know EXACTLY what they are for, but still even then not really because Hector's included and his hands are always soaking in jam or snot or dribble.

A rap song comes on and we all pretend we know the words, using the wires and plugs like microphones. Taking turns to make the other ones laugh.

Why do all rappers have to go on about how good they are the entire time? I've learned even from my experience with Mum, that when you down-play yourself and don't be dramatic, like I am not being this summer, sometimes others warm to you more. I well love rap music but I just wonder a bit why they don't just chill out a bit . . . be a bit more realistic?

'Pops, quick!' I leap up. 'Pass me some paper and a pen, quick!'

'Can't you just get the paper yourself?'

'Fine.'

I begin to write, on top of the music playing from the radio, some new lyrics from the character of a rapper, who is a bit more honest, a bit more humble.

THE HUMBLE RAPPER

Yo, yo, it's me, the humble rapper.

I'm kind of good but other rappers are better

talking numbers, maybe five out of ten,

possibly six, then again . . .

depends who's countin'.

Over hip hop, I spit bars and rap.

It's my most favourite thing after popping bubble
    wrap.

I write about normal things like what's on TV,

'bout Cheddar cheese and milky tea,

about the daily struggles of life

    for me

like wet sleeves and when

    food stuck in your teeth.

Jeeez . . .

I got a best friend, his name is Dave,

he's as tough as bricks and safe as a spade.

A proper legend, a diamond geezer,

got my back from all the jealous haters.

(I've actually only met Dave the once, it was a

    brief encounter,

in the shopping centre, on the escalator,

I shouted, 'Oi, Dave, you'd make a quite good

    best mate, bruv, gimme a ring!'

He said, 'I'll think about it, but I guess he never

    did.)

I'm the humble rapper.

Never going out of fashion,

I live in a massive mansion –

block of flats

with two goldfish

    and a three-legged

    cat.

If you opened my

    fridge you'd be sort of amazed –

I got bare fresh eggs, mayonnaise for days.

I got a TV, it works just fine

I got DVDs – most of them aren't mine.

My bed is as big as just a *double* bed.

I put my feet at the end and even have a

    pillow for my head,

And in my dreams I'm the best!

Ahead of the times – like my toothbrush is electric

And I would eat ice cream for

    breakfast . . . err . . . except I'm allergic.

I'm the humble rapper.

My biggest fan is my gran.

Sometimes she's away with the fairies,

she doesn't even know who I am.

But I don't get down in the dumps just cos
    she's old,
nuffin' a good rummage in the biscuit tin can't
    solve.
I got a car,
it's plastic and it fits in my hand.
I get around on the bus actually most days,
which is *pretty* convenient, the 137 stops just
    outside my place.
I-spy with my rapper eyes
something beginning with ME
in the library . . .
with a dictionary
Ooooooool
I'm a member. So. Yeah. It is likely.

I'm the humble rapper.
I have so much silver –
fillings in my teeth.
It's because I love
    cupcakes

and sour jelly sweets.

I love going on holiday to affordable retreats –
like the newsagent's at the top of my street.

I get a pedicure on my celebrity feet,
basically my cat licks my big toe about twice a
    week.

Is that disgusting? Yeah, maybe. Shouldn't say
    that out in public.

Awkward.

Moving forward . . .

I'm the humble rapper, a rapper that raps
rap, brap, blap, slap and all that.

I could find a rhyme for every letter
with an X on the map
but the poetry is the treasure, fancy that!

I've done only one show at the local coffee shop
but nobody really listened so I just gave up
but I did have hot chocolate in a takeaway cup,
marshmallows . . . err . . . HELLO!

Until I nearly burned the roof of my mouth off

and got told to shut up.

I guess not everybody loves hip hop.

Shamel

But don't hate the player, son, hate the rapping

   game.

I'm the humble rapper.

I earn money every week

from my 9 to 5 job at the bake-ry

where I give a rap for every cheese wrap that I

   make,

iced bun, doughnut, apple turnover, cake –

in your face!

I get sent free things in the post

like deliveries for my neighbours if they're not

   in – but I try not to boast.

I have more than most,

even a personal assistant but . . .

she's a ghost.

I'm the humble rapper

and I'm OK at rapping.

I'm medium-ish height and OK attractive.

My voice is all right, a little bit annoying.

I know some celebrities but no one worth knowing.

I have some hobbies, mostly knitting and sewing,

linking the thread of words with the fabric of a
    beat,

hitting the streets

until my trainers fall apart

not because I speak unique.

Because . . . well . . . this is art.

I'm the humble rapper,

rapping honestly,

about the muddy pigeons and
    grey weather that I see,

flying like a buzzing beat, stinging
    like a bumble,

chicks crowding me like a honey pot, homemade
    crumble,

taste the sincerity, taste the pudding, humble.

Probably by now you've got the cooker of your
  heart warming to me.
That's right, this rapper you can book for free in
  any neighbourhood
because I'm the humble rapper and I'm
  medium-ish not really any good.

I read it to Hector and Poppy and they laugh their
heads off and we speak to Will online
and I do it for him. He laughs his
head off too and says he wishes he
could come home now – *he's had
enough,* he says, and I play it cool
and say nothing but really I'm
thinking, *I've had enough of you
being away too.* He looks weird
and super faraway on the screen: he has freckles all
over his face and the sky is all clear there and fantastic.
Hector gets over-excited and tries to do a moonie and
pull his bum out and Will laughs even harder. Will
then shows us where he's staying at his aunt's house.

The houses in Spain are much more different, all white and stony and the furniture is much more colourful. It's so holiday-ish you can even smell the sun cream through the screen.

'Have you done your Superman?'

'Oh yeah! I smashed that one on the first day!' He beams proudly. 'I'm doing WAY more tricks than that now.'

WOW. Will's challenge was to throw his body into the air on a bike and he did it the first day . . . All I had to do was not be dramatic and it's a daily struggle. HUMPH.

I don't want to say goodbye.

'Home soon,' he says.

'Home soon,' I say back, smiling. I don't tell him about the fart in front of Madison or about being sick. I just say, 'See you soon.'

And he says, 'See you soon' too and then waves at us a big bye.

We shut the laptop screen.

Speaking to somebody over the internet is not real

life though, and part of me almost thinks it shouldn't be allowed to be that close to somebody and yet so far – it's fake, it's like an evil trick that messes with our brains.

I feel like Will's with us right now . . . but he's not.

'Right, what now?' Poppy bursts the dream bubble as soon as we've ended the call. 'What shall we do?'

'I know, I KNOW . . . let's persuade Mum to have a barbecue?'

'Yes, ask Mum,' Poppy squeals.

'You ask her.'

'But she'll say no.'

'Go on . . .'

'You do it, but try a new technique . . . firstly you have to use the word *barbie* like the grown-ups do. It looks like you know what you're talking about. And secondly, don't *ask* Mum to have a barbie, TELL her to have a barbie.'

'OK. I'll try.'

If I'm honest, seeing Will, even if just on the screen, has put a new spring in my step. Here goes nothing.

'Oi, Mum.'

'Don't *oi* me,' Mum snaps back. OOOOOOoooo. SOR-RY. I won't be *telling* her anything.

'Sorry, Mum.'

'It's OK, you're clearly over-excited about something. What's going on?'

'So maybe why don't you have a barbecue tonight and invite all your main friends down?'

'Darcy, you don't just *have* a barbecue, it takes planning – you've got to get all the bits and pieces.'

'We have all the *bits and pieces*.'

'We don't.'

'We have tomato sauce and bread and frozen things that we can warm up.'

'We don't have cheese squares. I don't even think we have charcoal for a barbecue.' Mum stares at me for a second.

I stare back. With my hugest most puppy-dog eyes. 'Please?'

'Yuck. Don't do those eyes with me, they don't work. I'll have a think and speak to your dad.'

That probably means a yes but I don't know because we don't very often get what we ask for.

'It could be nice, I suppose, to have a few people over, like a little housewarming?'

YES! My heart jumps out my rib-cage on a little parachute and dangles into my belly because I ADORE BARBECUES!

'I could always speak to Marnie?' Mum goes on. She's folding up Hector's best T-shirt. It has an ice cream on it with a scary face of a monster popping out of the ice cream and a lizard tail. It's fun.

'Marnie?'

'About inviting Donald over.'

NOOOOO! Not Donald. OH NOOOOOO OOO. NO. NO. NO. But I have to hold it together and complete my challenge and NOT be dramatic, just like how Will managed to smash his.

'OK.' I grumpily let the word spill out.

'You know the poor sausage will just be sitting in on his own playing computer games and being bored out of his brain.'

'He is SUCH a sausage – I dunno about a *poor* one, but a sausage is a very accurate comparison,' I say back.

'It won't hurt to have the poor sausage over for a sausage, will it?' Mum jokes.

I've started to see how a little less drama from my end certainly makes others respond better to my wishes. I think maybe this no-drama way of life could be a surprisingly positive one.

'Your rap is dumb,' Donald says with his stupid black eyes. 'It's a *joke*.' He looks like a panda bear.

'It's *meant* to be a *joke*. It's hydronic,' I fire back.

'Are you meaning to say I-RON-IC?' Donald smarms, all smarmy lip-balmy.

'No,' I lie. 'Hydronic is a new word for when you are being funny and hyper and hysterical and clever too, mixed in with science at the same time,' I bark back.

'Yeah, well it seems like perhaps you could be telling porkies to me because I've never heard of that word and I go to a really expensive school for child geniuses.'

'I wasn't telling porkies because if I was you'd probably eat them all up with bread and ketchup before I could tell them, you big fatso watso.'

'You called me fat! I'm telling Mum.'

'You called my lyrics dumb so what do you think about that?'

'DUMB. Did you not listen?' He puts a finger to his head and twists it.

'Guys, guys.' Timothy tries to quiet us down. His mum has dumped him on us too. Honestly, it's like our house is the crèche or something.

'Darcy, I'd be careful if I was you. Everybody knows you have a moustache.'

'No, I do absolutely not. I WISH I had one!'

'You do! And a beard is beginning to grow too!'

'Stop fighting!' Poppy screams.

'I wasn't fighting.'

'Darcy started it.'

'Oh, you liar.'

'Hey, shall we make some menus for the barbecue?' Poppy suggests to change the subject.

Mum stopped buying us all craft-box things or anything like that because we can't keep all the things nice and tidy inside and it goes everywhere, but Poppy always secretly asks for that sort of stuff for her birthday and keeps it all good and neat and nicely.

'I'll get my good bits if you stop fighting.'

'OK, fine.' That's a fair swap.

Donald, the panda sausage, stares at me all evil eyes. OH, GO AWAY, BEAR HEAD.

Poppy comes back with a big plastic carrier fulled with pens and felts and glitter and glue to make the menus for the barbecue. 'OK, no losing anything, don't rub the glue too much,' she worries, 'and put the right lid on the right pen.' She is trying to not be stressed about it but she can't help it. 'You see, that

noise that just camed out when you press the felt down, that means because you're pressing *too* hard, and on the pencil – look, you'll break the lead if you push down like that, you have to shade more to the side,' she bosses. 'Don't blend the yellow felt on the black – look, you'll make all black get on the nib.'

I look round and Hector's just had enough of being obedient and has glued himself and Lamb-Beth up like glittery clouds. They both look too cute and amazing for me to tell them off.

'I don't know what to write – what's even on the menu?' Timothy asks.

'That's a point,' I agree.

'Shall we just write normal barbecue things?' Poppy suggests. 'Burgers. Kebabs.'

'Yes, that sounds good.'

'We can make the prices funny things instead of money?' Hector offers. 'Like a funny face for a hot dog?'

'Ha-ha! Good idea!' I laugh. 'A song for a corn on the cob?'

'That will be me with all the corn then!' Donald snorts. 'I'll have the stuff growing out of my ears!'

'Huh? How come?' Timothy challenges him.

'Err . . . because I'm a gifted singer.'

I can't hold my laughter in, I snort a rude childish dribble. 'Can you actually sing, Donald?'

'You bet I jolly well can! My mum says I have the voice of an angel.'

We all look at each other. Trying to hold our opinions in. Because if it's one thing we know, it's that Marnie says A LOT of things.

I wish Will was here. He would be so fun to have here right now and would be making me laugh so much. I can't wait for him to come back from his holiday – it feels like he has been gonned for roughly one hundred years. It really, truly does.

The sky begins to skulk and slip away, the bright orange button of sun is dipping down and a cool stream of evening creeps out over the garden.

The other adults pour in. Marnie, John and Dad. Even Timothy's mum stops by for a burger.

And just as I hoped, the warm smoky clouds of hot coals begin to float in the air, whipping the sky up and making the belly rumble and the neighbours jealous. There's bowls of salad and multi-coloured rainbow vegetables and fruits piled high into gorgeous bowls with creamy coleslaw and lashings of chivey peppered potato salad and every condiment and shiny glazed bread rolls and toasty pittas and delicious warm baguettes. There are crispy good jacket potatoes with yellow squares of melty butter and salty crystals and towers of plump corn on the cobs and kebabs made

with peppers and halloumi, the most blessed plastic salty rubber magic cheese in the world.

Dad turns burgers with a flip of the tongs, happy, with a beer in his hand.

I overhear Marnie chewing Timothy's mum's ear off about Timothy's performing arts weekend school thing.

'My boy Donald is *stunning* at performance,' I hear Marnie saying to her. 'He did a school play last year – he played a frog. His ribbit was so authentic, you know, so realistic I thought there was an actual real-life frog in the school hall. I kid you not. Absolutely amazing,' she says, absolutely so chuffed with herself and her little glass of pink fizz. 'And he's never even met a

frog properly, has he, John?' she says to Donald's dad, John, and he nods while biting into his cheeseburger.

'Donald dear, why

don't you show us some of your drama? Or your musical theatre . . . or . . . I mean . . . he might be too shy . . . but Donald dear, why don't you show the gang your singing?'

Oh, here we go. Please, no.

'Mother!' he shrieks. 'I don't want to.'

'Oh, go on, Donald, it would be selfish of me to keep my son's angelic talents to himself.' She slurps her drink and a kiss of coral lipstick smears the side of the glass. 'I'll buy you a treat tomorrow.'

'Swear?' Donald warns.

'Swear,' Marnie replies.

And Donald takes a big deep breath in . . . closes his eyes and tips his pig snout back. And what can only be described as opera came out from that barrel of a boy. He sang in a language I didn't understand which made the moment even more magical and surreal. It was beautiful, cinematic, emotional, a choirboy song that was everything Donald was not. Gentle, touching, powerful, stunning.

Wow.

His arms and fingers moved so softly in the time, like he was a feather, falling so gracefully. We were *all* transfixed.

'Whoa,' Timothy mumbled in our ears. 'That boy can SANG!'

And he really most truly could. And when he finished we didn't even really clap at first. We was all just mostly simply blown away. Completely grateful for what we had just witnessed. When Donald finished he shook his head and shrugged.

'Sorry,' he grunted, as though what he'd just done was an accident.

And we all clapped him. Hard.

I think it could possibly be my all-time favourite thing when somebody is so good at something you just don't expect of them. It really is wonderful. I can't help but think Donald might be a bit secretly cool now. WOW.

We go to bed with fulled-up tummies to the absolute brim. I am bursting with delicious flavours. Poppy *and* Hector are both in my double bed again but I don't mind one tiny bit. Lamb-Beth is sleeping on the landing because unfortunately she still can't climb up

the stairs and Dad says he doesn't want us *carrying her up because it's not fair to take an animal up somewhere where they can't get back down again.*

I hear Poppy's little breathing and Hector's little dreaming.

The night sky is clear and navy and the orange gems of the streetlamps are bleeding gold into the sky. And I feel happy in this lovely new house of ours.

Chapter Sixteen

It's Dad's day of treating us to some fun activities. He has taken the day off and EVERYTHING! WHOOOP! We are so excited. We've been guessing all morning about where he's gonna take us. Theme park, build-a-bear workshop, the circus, a comic convention, chocolate factory . . . maybe an all-you-can-eat Chinese buffet perhaps? But right now . . . he's still asleep.

Come on, WAKE UP, DAD!

'Just five more minutes . . .' he mumbles, his face pressed all deep hard into the pillow, but I know that five minutes in sleep land rushes past as quick as a not stopping train.

At first we don't mind so much.

'Why don't we snuggle back into bed and you can read us one of your stories to pass the time until he wakes up?' Poppy asks.

'OK. I don't mind.'

'Bring Lamb-Beth up,' says Poppy.

'We aren't meant to.' Hector shakes his head. ''member?'

'Yeah, well, Dad isn't *meant* to be sleeping in on our FUN day.'

That's a true point. We scoop Lamb-Beth up and she silently flops into our arms and lets us carry her upstairs to my hot attic.

I open up the windows all big and the summer morning leaps in with the sound of singing birds and street sweepers. I am ready to read my story . . .

'All geva,' Hector says, squeezing into the middle of us, resting his head on my shoulder. 'An eldest one, an in-between one and a youngest one.'

Ha-ha. Poppy's the *in-between* one! I laugh at Hector's funny brain.

'Yes.' I grin. 'All together in Darcy's secret Angrosaurus rex dungeon.'

'It isn't a dungeon up here,' Hector disagrees. 'It's like a secret treehouse.'

This makes me laugh . . . and be happy. 'It IS like a secret treehouse.' Immediately it makes me love my room morer.

'You are still an Angrosaurus rex though!' Hector screams and giggles, hiding under the blankets because he knows I will pinch and tickle him until his skin crawls and we all bundle up in my bed and play-fight, laughing and squealing.

'Hey.' Hector stops, panting, out of breath. 'But wait a sec, yeah?'

'Yeah?' I say.

'Why don't you ever writted a story about us three, me and you and Poppy?'

'My name is actually Madison,' Poppy corrects, but she needs to know this name really isn't sticking. 'Because anyway Darcy doesn't need write a story about us, we are a story already. The best story in the whole world!' she screeches, arms in the sky, in her pink nightie, before she crashes onto our heads.

She is so right. We are a story.

'We can make one up now . . . ?' I offer.

'About a treehouse?'

'Yes.'

'And *the all* three of us?' Hector asks.

'Yes.'

'OK, let me . . .' Hector begins. 'Once uponed a

timed . . . ' He pauses and looks at me. 'Darcy, aren't
you going to writted this down?'

'Oh, sorry, of course.' I quickly grab a pen, trying
not to laugh, and he closes his
eyes and says, 'There
were three children
– all of them were
best friends and peas in
pods and brothers and sisters
and they always beed all ageva in

the loveliest attic treehouse telling stories and being so much friends as well with a lamb.'

'That's lovely, Hector!' I smile.

'My turn . . . my turn . . .' Poppy butts in. 'Once upon a time there was an attic in the heart of Miami and it looked like a treehouse and this really cool like amazing girl called . . . erm . . . Sydney Ray Melanie Summer opened up a hairdresser's salon and also a dance school inside the att—'

'NO!' Hector screams. 'Not always a Barbie story.'

'That's not a BARBIE, you really stupid boy!' Poppy yells back.

'Don't call me so stupid! It was a Barbie story and I EVEN know because you did it in an American accent and moved your hand all like that.' Hector bats his lashes and moves his hand all fast like a TV presenter.

'Like WHAT?'

'Like THISED!' He does it again, this time even more, and he *does* have a point. All Poppy's make-believe games are always set in the 'heart of Miami' and ALWAYS feature a *Sydney* or a *Megan* or a *Summer*. It does get rather tiresome.

'Well, YOUR story was all lovey-dovey brothers and sisters.'

'Well, I changing mine story NOW!' Hector yells. 'Darcy, write this, OK . . . Once uponed a timed there was a horrible scary UGLY witch girl living in a haunted treehouse even ALL BY HER OWN SELF and she had to eat slugs and worms and poo chocolate bars and the only smell was farts and it was always raining and her name was POPPY!'

'I'm telling!' Poppy roars in Hector's face.

'OK, OK, calm down . . . calm down . . . I'm going to tell a story . . .' I say. 'It's OK . . . my turn . . .'

'But she was really a mean girl to me.' Hector dribbles and crocodile tears.

'WHAT ARE YOU TALKING ABOUT, YOU ABSOLUTE BRATTY MUSHROOM CRAB? You are the horrid one that made up a mean spiteful story about me!'

It's no use, I just begin . . .

While I read, Poppy gets out her little 'friendship bracelets' craft box and begins plaiting . . .

> THREE LITTLE BIRDS WITHOUT A HOME
>
> Once upon a time there were three little birds
> without a home.

'Wait . . . why didn't they have a home?' Poppy interjects.

'I'm just about to tell you if you wait,' I say, but really I hadn't thought of the reason, but now I have so the story may continue . . . 'I'll start again.'

> Once upon a time there were three little
> happy birds. They loved their lives very much.
> They played in the lake, sucked plump juicy
> worms from the ground and sunbathed in the
> warm grass.

One day there was a terrible storm and all the birds rushed back to their nests that sat perched in the trees, and hid away until the storm passed.

But the three little birds could not find their nest. It was nowhere to be seen.

'Where has our lovely nest gone?' the little bird said, his wings up around his head like a scarf.

'It seems to have blown away in the storm,' the eldest bird said.

'We have to hide somewhere or we will get blown away!' said the in-between bird. 'Where will we go now?'

The wind picked up quickly and was howling and moving them along. 'Don't worry, little ones, we will find somewhere,' the eldest said. 'I'm sure Mr Squirrel will let us in.'

And the birds flew the best they could against the powerful sucking wind, against the furious pellets of raindrops that fell like water bombs.

Mr Squirrel's Walnut House was nice and safe and lined in purple velvet. The heating was always on and chestnuts were *always* roasting. They were looking forward to getting cosy and warm, nestling into his soft armchairs and snuggling up for a little doze.

They banged on the door as loud as they could (while still being polite) and waited for Mr Squirrel to let them inside.

'Hello?' he shouted from inside the comfort of

his giant Walnut House.

'It's the three little birds – our lovely nest seems to have blown away in the storm, we have nowhere to go,' said the eldest bird.

'Please let us inside to shelter from the storm,' added the in-between bird – she never minded being outspoken.

'Oh, I'm afraid I don't have the room. I could maybe squeeze ONE of you in but never all three of you.'

'Please, we are only small,' the youngest bird added.

'Afraid not,' said Mr Squirrel. 'One or none.'

This angered the eldest bird. Mr Squirrel had PLENTY of room in his Walnut House but he was just too selfish and too greedy. The sky was grey now and swimming in a wet newspapery smeary mud. The swelling clouds were thundering and dangerous, the branches beneath them were trembling angrily. They could feel the warmth of the Walnut House breathing out from beneath the door, smell the rich sweet smell of toasting nuts.

The eldest bird looked at her baby brother and sister. 'Go on, baby bird, go inside Mr Squirrel's house and warm up and have some sweet hot chestnuts.'

'No,' said the youngest baby bird. 'We stick together. Where you go, I go. We are three peas in a pod.'

And the three birds turned down Mr Squirrel's offer and, soaking wet, flapped away.

'Where now?' asked the youngest bird.

'We could try Fatty Owl – he was always nice and let us in for barbecued reeds,' replied the eldest bird.

The hissing rain flattened their tiny heads, their wings were heavy with the weight of the water. Fatty Owl was a little further away but they knew *he* would let them in. He always did.

'Yo! You guys? Waddup? You guys cray cray out here in a storm like this.'

'Please, Fatty Owl, our nest got blown away in the storm – can we come and dry off inside your Beehive Barn?' asked the eldest of the birds, shivering.

'Ah, no can do. SORRY, DUDES!' he said from his Beehive Barn hidden in the trees. 'I'm making barbecued jerk reeds, it just takes up a lot of space. YOLO!'

'But please . . .' said the in-between bird. 'We can help you.' Barbecued reeds were her favourite.

'OK, I got space for one of you. But not ALL of you.'

The eldest looked at her baby brother and sister. It was getting darker and darker – soon it would be harder to find somewhere to make a shelter for the night. At least to know one of the three birds was safe and warm would be better than none of them.

'Go on.' She nudged the in-between bird on the shoulder. 'I know how much you love barbecued reeds, and I will come back and get you as soon as I have somewhere for the three of us to be.'

'No way!' replied the in-between bird. 'I'd rather never eat another bite of barbecued jerk reeds again than be without my brother and sister. We are three peas in a pod.' And she folded her wings and turned her beak away.

And the three birds flew on to their final option (with the in-between bird mumbling some VERY rude words about Fatty Owl under her breath).

Betty Bat always had a space for everybody in her home. Made from a recycled suitcase that was wedged in between two big trunks high in the trees, her home was always warm, always waterproof and very spacious.

'Betty Bat, it's us, the three birds. Our nest has been blown away in the storm – may we please come in for the night?'

But Betty Bat pretended to be blind and deaf and acted as though she lost her memory too.

'Errr . . . I think I left the chocolate spread in the mountain,' she garbled, to sound completely confused and avoid letting the three helpless birds in.

'Betty? Please.' And a furious strike of white lightning bolted through the grey sky. The ground, a slick of mud. The birds were hopeless and terrified. Betty heard the lightning but she was too selfish.

'Errrmmm . . .' Betty the Bat decided to avoid confrontation and just play dumb. 'Is the salad dressing gluten-free? Yes please, I'll take one ticket to Switzerland,' she lied.

'Come on, guys. We will find a way. We always do,' said the eldest bird solemnly.

The night was long and wet and cold. The sky was black and unforgiving. The three little birds had never felt more sad and blue, like the world had turned its back on them. They huddled up into the crook of a tree trunk and tried to sleep, even though they were absolutely freezing cold, shivering and starving hungry. They managed to fall asleep to the repetitive sound of falling rain and cuddled in each other's arms.

The next day, the sky was clear and dry, the world was right again. The eldest led her siblings to the hot springs for a warm soak. While they bathed she plucked them juicy worms from the ground and fed them pears and camomile tea from a petal. When they were fed and warmed up the determined eldest decided that they were going to build a new nest. A nest that would be a BAJILLION MILLION times better than the last! This one would be waterproof *and* stormproof *and* cosy *and* strong *and* unbreakable!

It would be the best house ever.

They flew up to the biggest, most wonderful tree they could find and began to plot where

their new home would be. The honey sun was watching them, smiling on their backs. So were the jealous eyes of their neighbours. *What were these three little birds up to?*

But when the eldest bird began to scale the trunk of the tree her beak began to jolt, judder and peck. A big hole was instantly carved into the trunk in no time at all.

'Huh?' She was confused and tried again. More wood chiselled away from the tree trunk, leaving a big gawping hole in the face of the tree. 'No way.' She flapped and clapped her wings. *Could this be true?*

She beckoned her brother and sister up to help her. 'Try this . . .' she said, and waited to see if their beaks did the same. And just as the eldest had done moments before, both the little birds' beaks sawed the wood in the same way.

'Guys!' the eldest said. 'I think we might be woodpeckers!'

'Woodpeckers? No! We are just normal scruffy birds,' said the in-between bird.

'No, we are! We are woodpeckers and everybody knows that woodpeckers make the best nests ever!'

The eldest bird jumped up and flapped her

wings in joy. She was over the moon! She circled
and spun and hugged her brother and sister and
they laughed too. They all couldn't wait to use
their beaks to make a home.

They would be building an amazing nest in no
time!

'What are those *crazy* birds doing?' Mr
Squirrel asked Fatty Owl.

'Who knows? Them lot are coo-coo loco cray-
cray!'

But oh, they knew, when the three little birds'
treehouse was built. When the beautiful trunk of
the best, most amazing tree made space for the
most incredible ornate palace. They built doors
and windows, pillars and balconies, they built a
bedroom each and a big playroom. Slanted
rooftops for the rain to patter off and even a
drainage system! They made a little pool of their
own for swimming, hammocks to relax in and a
watchtower to spy for danger (and spotting big
juicy worms!). Their treehouse was paradise. A

place where white elderflowers floated into the
windows, pears from the tree next door would
grow into it so the woodpecking birds could bite
into the flesh whenever they fancied. They
stuffed their warm heaven with bundles of sticks
and leaves and made glorious beds from cotton

and fallen feathers. It was the greatest treehouse ever.

'We did it!' they cried, and they huddled together. Hugging and high-fiving and celebrating.

Until a week later, back came the horrendous storm. This time it was even worse than the last. It ripped the trees bare, stripping the branches naked. The sky grunted and grumbled and the navy clouds swirled and attacked the forest as though it had never been attacked before. The rain fell like an ocean. The forest was doomed . . .

'Do you hear something?' the eldest bird asked her little sister, who was filing her claws with a fruit stone.

'PLEASE!' cried the voices from outside. It was Mr Squirrel, Fatty Owl and Betty Bat, howling at the door.

'Hang on . . .' The eldest bird went to the door. 'Hi, Mr Squirrel. Hello, Fatty Owl. You all right, Betty Bat – do you know where you are?'

'Yes!' Betty Bat cried. 'Of course I know where I am! In the middle of a blooming thunderstorm, that's WHERE! My Suitcase got blown away in the storm! MY Suitcase! It had all my lovely things inside it and now it is gone!' It made the eldest bird laugh to know that Betty's memory was all there now!

'And me too!' hooted Fatty Owl. 'That horrible storm came and blew away my Barn. I spent so long building that. It took all my recipe books and special barbecue marinades with it! Now I have nothing!'

'Me too!' wailed Mr Squirrel. 'The awful storm came out of nowhere and sent my beautiful Walnut House rolling down the hill! Please, can we stay with you, just for the night, to dry off in the warmth?'

The eldest bird could not believe what she was hearing. She looked at her three desperate neighbours. The eldest called her baby brother and sister to the door.

'So *now* you want our help?' she asked.
'After you saw us suffer. You all lied and said
there wasn't enough space or enough food to
go round when you knew we all had nothing.'

'Oh, forgive me!' pleaded Betty Bat. 'I am
blind and deaf, remember? I didn't know it
was the three of you, or of COURSE I would
have let you in,' she lied.

'I don't want your excuses. I am just going
to treat you the same way you treated us,' the
eldest said.

'Yes,' added the in-between bird. 'Only ONE
of you can come in to keep out of the storm.'

'Well, obviously, it should be ME!' screeched
Mr Squirrel. 'Everybody needs toasted nuts on
a stormy night like this!'

'Listen, mate,' said the in-between bird.
'I didn't realize there even WAS a storm
until now, as our home is SO well insulated!'
This only made the three neighbours shiver
more.

'Y'all know we go way back!' said Fatty
Owl. 'I can show you how to make barbecue
marinade — it's your favourite, isn't it?'

'Not any more!' the in-between bird replied.

'Choose me!' raved Betty Bat. 'I will make
you so much blueberry pie you won't be able to
see the wood for the trees!'

'I thought you couldn't see or hear anything
anyway? Or was that a lie?' the eldest bird
snubbed.

And immediately the three neighbours
began to squabble and fight. They argued
and scraped, attacking each other.

Well, this just absolutely infuriated the
eldest of the birds. Suddenly she found that
her patience had just about gone. She was
terribly sick of being kind and polite and
caring and she'd had enough.

Just as she was just about ready to go
crazy at these three meanies and lose her
temper like an absolute terradaptor

Angrosarus rex, her little brother and sister looped their arms into her wings and said, 'They aren't worth the drama. Just be happy and calm as you always are. Two wrongs don't make a right.'

And the eldest bird knew they were right, so she composed herself. She knew that with her brother and sister she was the strongest, luckiest creature in all the trees combined.

These neighbours were not worth the outburst, they were not worth the drama.

Luckily for the three neighbours, the birds were not as heartless as them. They decided to let them inside their treehouse to keep

warm and safe until the storm passed. In heaped blankets, they dried off and snoozed. They shared roasted chestnuts and barbecued reeds and spicy cauliflower and there was lots of blueberry pie for everybody.

And in the morning, when the sky was
clear and the world was right, the three
neighbours thanked the birds so much for their
kindness.

And the three woodpecking birds decided
they could do something even kinder and use
their new talents to build Mr Squirrel, Fatty
Owl and Betty Bat a home each. Because
kindness, unlike nuts or barbecued reeds or
blueberry pie . . . or even space . . . NEVER
runs out.

'You're the best, Darcy.' Poppy links my arm.

'No,' I say, 'you two are.'

'No, we ALLED are. Three birds,' Hector says.

'That's it.' I couldn't agree more. 'Three birds.'

And then Poppy hands us each a little friendship
bracelet she made us. She blushes when she hands
them to us. They are rainbow-coloured with a little

bead attached to them. It's SO cool. Poppy NEVER does no-reason presents like this. We both put the bracelets on, admiring them on our arms.

'Don't get too excited,' she jokes. 'I can take these away just as quickly as I gave them out.'

Chapter Seventeen

'Dad's STILL not wide awake even yet!' Poppy rolls her eyes.

We then trot downstairs and make some scrummy crumpets although we ran out of butter so our only spread option was peanut butter. We aren't stupid, we know if we bring Dad a coffee in bed it's a double bonus because you are not only waking Dad up but he can't be mad at you either because you've made him a coffee so if anything you're in his extra excellent books. But this is the THIRD coffee we've taken in and the other ones have gone all cold and ugly-looking. We don't make him any crumpets because we want them all for our own self. I stomp in loud this time, and Poppy and I are nudging each other, whispering, 'You wake him up.' 'No, you do it.' 'I did it last time.' 'You.' 'You.' *Snore, snore, bore.*

Fine.

I know as I am the oldest it is YET again down to me to create our own fun.

'Shall we go and make a fun brilliant cake?'

'Yes!' Poppy says. 'Then we can wake Dad up, naturally, with the great smell of cake.'

'OK. Good idea.'

'Wait, first I need a wee.'

'Me too.'

'Can't you wait?'

'You go in the bin.'

'I can't, it's made of straw.'

'Oh, it's fine, it will collect all the wee, no problem.'

'OK, if you're sure.'

It doesn't collect all the wee at all. Poppy's wee drizzles absolutely everywhere. We have to use toilet roll to clean it up, but somehow the toilet roll breaks

and we use more and more. We decide to do one last check on Dad's waking up.

'Pssst. Dad. Dad. Wake up and take us to Pizza Hut.'

'I'm not asleep, I'm just resting my eyes.'

'Well, can you stop? You did say you would treat us today.'

'It's my day off, Darcy, I'm allowed a lie-in.'

'Hm. It might be your day off but it's our day *on*.'

'What time is it?'

I look at the clock behind him. It's 6.02 a.m. I didn't realize it was *quite* that early. What can I say? We were excited.

'It's seven thirty,' I lie.

'What? Darcy, at least let me sleep until eight! Nowhere will even be open. Have some breakfast.'

'We already did!'

'OK. I'll get up in a minute.'

For a sec the bed looks so cosy and I think about getting deep inside the blankets with the

sleeping bears that are Mum and Dad, but can I be bothered with Mum's sour sweaty armpit smell and Dad's hideous pooey morning breath? Probs not.

Anyway. We've got work to do. We're going to make a cake.

'Poppy,' I announce in the living room, 'we have to turn forward all the clocks and make them look like they are all seven thirty a.m.' Lamb-Beth looks at me like I'm mad and closes her eyes back to sleep. Probably a good idea.

'Huh? Why?'

'Becaused I lied to Dad and told him it was seven thirty when it's actually six a.m. in the morning.'

'Six?'

'We've been awake for ages, that means.'

'It's because it's so sunny outside and the birds and everything.'

And before I can even turn round Hector smashes a pillow into my face. 'WAR!' he cries.

AARGGGGGGHHHHHHHHHHHHHHH!

And Poppy jumps on my back and starts beating me over the head with Hector's teddy bear.

'Traitor!' I squeal, and begin fighting them both, whipping a giant cushion over their heads. They laugh and fight back. Poppy then pulls out the sofa seats and uses the arm of the sofa like a launch pad surfboard, sailing into the sky. She lands, clattering, against the TV, which wobbles and nearly knocks over but doesn't smash, thankfully. Hector then picks up the other sofa seat bit, which covers his whole body

– he can barely even wrap his tiny hands around the edges. He looks like a massive walking slice of toast, and like a shield he rams towards us. Toppling me over backwards. We rip all the cushions off all the chairs, laughing so hard we can barely contain ourselves. *Snig. Snig. Hee. Hee. Ha. Ha. Hoo. Sh . . . Ha!* And then we remember that one of the sofas is a sofa bed!

OOOOHHHHHHHH YES!

A new game is, naturally, instantly invented. We take turns to lie down on the sofa and be rolled inside the sofa bed. The metal frame is squashed around our bodies but it doesn't hurt because the mattress soft bit cosies you all up like a Swiss-roll cake. Then the other two have to squish down with all their might to try and roll you into the sofa. The aim is that you'll be able to feel the feeling of being completely immersed and flattened into the sofa bed like a panini being cooked in a toastie maker. Perhaps we will get so skilled at it that one day we can fold in, have the whole family sit on top of us like an actual real-life

sofa and then spring out all by our own selves like surprising human jack-in-a-boxes!

That would be great.

But then, just exactly like every game we play:

'MUM!' Hector screams. 'MUM!' He's trapped his finger in the metal bracket hinge bit.

'Shhhhh!' I say. 'Be quiet.'

'MUM!' he roars again.

'MUM!'

'Hector, shhh. You'll wake them up.'

'My finger though, my finger.'

'It's fine. Look, do you want to put a chocolate bar in the microwave?'

Tears immediately dry up.

'Yeah. OK.' He nods. Stupid crocodile-tear baby.

We don't have ANY chocolate bars.

'We don't have any chocolate bars, Hector.'

'You said we were making a brilliant cake.' Oh yeah. Oh yeah. OK.

I even drag a chair to the top cupboard and look inside there for a secret stash of chocolate as Mum sometimes has to hide the confectionery to keep it away from us crazy Gremlin monster children.

'We don't have any chocolate.'

'But you *said*.'

'Well, if I said we were going up in space tomorrow would you believe me?'

'Maybe.'

'Idiot.'

'OK, what do we need for a cake? Flour.'

'Is it self-raising?'

'I don't know. Cakes raise, so that one, I guess.'

'Eggs.'

'We don't have any eggs – will...cream cheese do?'

'Yeah, maybe.'

'You need butter. This pack is covered in bits of toast.'

'Scrape them off.'

'I don't think there's enough.'

I think we need to forget about a cake.

'What about this?' Poppy pulls out an almost antique-looking packet of orange jelly. There is dust all wrapped around it, it's fluffy.

'Yes! Jelly!' I clap.

'Jelly! I love jelly!' Hector claps too, the gaps in his teeth give him a lisp. It's too late, now he's seen it, he will HAVE to have it.

'Where did you find that, Poppy?' I ask.

'Up here.'

'Oh, gross, do you think that was left from the people that lived here before?'

'Must be. It's out of date, I think.'

'Surely jelly can't go OFF, it's jelly. It's the next thing to plastic.'

There was me NOT wanting to find anything left over from the previous people that lived here before us, and now I am SO grateful!

'What are the instructions?'

'Can't read them, they're all covered in fur and gunk.'

''K, well, it defo needs to melt, so just throw it in the microwave. The microwave can cook even anything.'

'All right then.'

We unwrap the jelly, peeling it out of its crackling casing. We stare at it. Prod it. Lick it. It's soft and hard and bright orange like a traffic light.

'Wait, we need the bit that makes it into a shape – the mould thingy.'

'What thing?'

'You know, the plastic rabbit-shaped thing that the jelly goes into?'

'Oh yes, the yellow plastic thing.'

'Yes, it's what makes the jelly into a rabbit shape. Once it's melted you put it in the fridge to chill and it comes out in a rabbit shape.'

'Yes. Must be up here with all the cake tins.'

''K, have a look.'

'Hold my legs then so I don't wobble off.'

'I am.'

'Hold tighterer.'

'Gosh, it stinks up here of old naans.'

'Bleugh.'

'Oh, look, a cupcake tray.'

'Hey, bring that down for tomorrow – leave it out so Mum gets the hint.'

'Here it is!'

'Show me!'

'Yes!'

'That'll do.'

'Rinse it out. It looks like Mum just packed all this

stuff without cleaning it. It's all dusty.'

We rinse the yellow bunny-shaped jelly mould out. We can't find a tea towel so we dry it on our pyjamas. Then we dollop the jelly into the body of the jelly mould. Then shove the whole thing into the microwave.

'How long for?'

'I'm not sure – maybe an hour?'

'Sounds about right. Most things usually take an hour, don't they?'

We shove the jelly in the micro-wave and decide to get ready for the day while the jelly cooks. When it comes out it will be like one big lovely jelly sweet.

'Morning, kids!' It's Dad. He's woked up as a

monster and chases us around the hall and kitchen, scooping us up and tickling us so we laugh like hyenas. Poppy and Hector get tipped upside down but I don't as much because I'm more heavier now and feel a bit fat in places actually, but I don't let that upset me and just happily wait my turn to be tickled.

'Thanks for my coffees! All three of them!' He laughs.

'Did you love them?' Poppy asks, quite reasonably.

'They were all cold. I have to make a new one.'

'Sorry about that.'

'You guys go and get ready and I'll make a coffee and jump in the shower.'

YES! YES! YES! A whole day of being with Dad and having a great laugh. Which is fabulous, because I was a bit worried it was going to end up like the day when Mum promised us the zoo which turned out to just be chaos.

BANG!

BANG!

BANG!

BANG!

'What the—?' Dad shouts. We smell it before we see it. Hot, thick lava. Plastic, melting, yellow and orange sun river, like an alien, gloopy, snotty, sticky, custardy, molten, sicky flood. And the microwave is black. Splattered, explosion of charcoal steam and electric burning. The powder soot smoke stains creeping up the wall. The wire burned out. The smell is thick, cloggy, plastic, plastering up our noses and retching the back of our throats. Mum is pounding down the stairs, wrapping her dressing gown around her.

Dad is so angry he just shouts at us to get out and go away. Then he picks up the whole microwave quickly and boots it out into the garden where it singes in the grass. I don't think he was meant to touch it.

His face is so angry like a dangerous livid animal. We all stand together – Poppy, Hector and I – in a tiny small crowd, trying to hide like tincy crumbs.

All Dad can say to us in his rage is, 'You lied about the time! It's so early!'

And we creep up to our room. Far away from the rancid smell of burnt microwave, mushroom clouds of black smoke, crystallized sugar and melted plastic.

Chapter Eighteen

We have camed to the Adventure Playground to get out of the smoke-filled in-trouble house. We all have our tails very in-between our legs because we got SO in trouble about the microwave and Mum said it was Dad's fault because he didn't wake up with us. But really, it was definitely OUR fault. We all know that.

It turns out I don't know if I like the Adventure Playground as much as I thought. I mean, if I wanted an assault course, I'd go on one. It's like training for the *army*! The slides are all really tall and winding and scary and the ladders go on and on and on. There's this one tyre on a rope that slides along, except only all cool-looking growed-up kids that all know each other's names are queuing up to go on it and I don't want to look a fool in front of them. I can't lose my insecurities and be myself like how I used to in the park and pretend I live in the jungle or whatever. So I just sit by Dad on the bench while he reads his book. I watch a dog sniffing another dog's bum. The other dog doesn't seem to mind it either, weirdos.

Poppy and Hector play in the smallerer park and Poppy loves it because she can do *everything* and

has basically become the superhero of the baby park, gliding along the monkey bars, whooshing down the slide, swinging kids off the roundabout, bouncing on the seesaw. Showing off. And I can't participate, even though I want to. In case the big kids from the tyre swing see me having a laugh with the little ones.

Four weeks into the holidays and it feels as though my life has not progressed in the slightest. At least Will is back soon.

'Hi,' says a voice. I turn round. It's this boy with lots of little plaits like worms and glasses. 'Want to play airports?'

'How old are you?' I ask?'

'Eight and three quarters.'

WAY TOO YOUNG, plus besides I hate it when kids say 'three quarters'.

You're not eight and three quarters. It's not cute. It's annoying and you are eight. Just eight.

'I have a sister that might want to play airports,' I say back and call Poppy over.

She pants towards us. 'Wassup?'

'Want to play airports with this kid who's eight?'

'And three quarters,' he adds.

'Whatever.'

'Sure. I'll play. Let me get Hector.'

'I have my cousins here too. Maybe they can play.'

Nobody told me there were *others*.

'If we pretend this is the terminal and this is the check-in bit?'

'Hey, the roundabout can be the carousel where you collect your luggage off?'

'OK. Cool.'

I watch Poppy and Hector begin to bond and play. Dad watches me watching them.

'Why don't you join in, D?' He nudges me. He is reading a book with a blue cover – it looks hard to read. 'You like to play too.'

'No I don't! Not baby games,' I want to snap, but I need to keep my calm. I've been doing so well at not being an Angrosaurus rex out in public (or anywhere, if I do say so myself).

He glances me a look. 'OK, fine.'

I get lumbered with the job of taking people's tickets when they board on the aeroplane. The aeroplane is the big slide. I don't have to do much so I don't mind. I just sit at the top of the slide. It's just a bit annoying because I can see Poppy and Hector chatting to 8 and ¾ and all his cousins all the way down there by the sandpit and I just have to be all here on my own waiting for when they decide in the game that it's time to board the plane.

'Are you getting on the aeroplane yet then?' I shout across, and 8 and ¾ has the audacity to shout back, 'We're just in Duty Free! Hold on!'

I'm thinking, *DUTY FREE*, it's a *GAME*. It's **IMAGINARY**. There is no Duty Free, for crying out loud sake. Still I wait. Like an overripe lemon. Watching the other kids in the playground let their hair dangle to the ground on the back of a swing, trip up on their Velcro-strap trainers, toddlers crying, ice

cream toppling off cones, mums shouting, dads laughing, mums laughing, dads shouting, nannies catching up with the old chitchat, and me. Alone. Waiting for people to get on my imaginary aeroplane like an absolute mug.

I'm well bored. I know what I'll do . . .

'This is the LAST FINAL call for MISS POPPY BURDOCK, HECTOR BURDOCK and ALL THOSE OTHER PEOPLE THEY ARE WITH!' I shout.

Poppy looks up, mortified, like I've bombed her life.

'I repeat!' I shout again. 'THAT THIS IS THE FINAL AND LAST CALL FOR ANY OTHER PASSENGERS FLYING!'

'No!' shouts Poppy. 'That's not fair, you didn't give us an even fair chance to get on or enjoy the airport!'

'It's not my fault that you're swanning about in Duty Free!'

'I didn't know the flight was about to take off.'

'Yeah, well, it is.'

'OK, quick! Guys! Come on!' Poppy shouts to everybody with a worried look on her face. 'We don't want to miss the flight.'

'Where is this flight going?' 8 and ¾ *just has* to get all involved, doesn't he?

'Italy,' I say.

'Oh no, that's not us. Don't worry, Poppy, we're getting on the flight to Egypt.'

'Oh, phew.' Poppy is relieved, like she's at a real actual airport and taking sides with this wormy-haired creep.

'This goes to Egypt too,' I say, all making it clear that I know best actually.

'We are a DI-RECT to Egypt,' he argues like I'm a two-year-old idiot, all spelling the sentence out.

'Oh, I beg your pardon, I'm sorry, I get muddled up because I do so many flights. Sorry, this *is* in fact the direct to Egypt and I know because I WORK here.'

'Really?' 8 and ¾ snottily looks the slide up and down. 'Are there first-class seats?'

This boy is really getting on my nerves. Poppy and Hector and ALL the other cousins start snobbishly looking down the slide too as though it's not to their taste. I feel myself beginning to take pride in the slide, embarrassed almost. *Why is it covered in leaves and graffiti?* It's MEANT to be a first-class aeroplane to Egypt!

'Of course, sir!' I smile.

'Very well then.' They hand me their tickets. The tickets are tissues that one of the cousins' mums had with them. I take them, thanking them as they pass. And then I just get the idea in my head to really show this 8 and ¾ who is boss, but I'm going to have to be clever about it, and I can't lose my temper as I normally would do as I refuse to break my no-drama challenge due to a duel with this little 8 and ¾. Play along . . .

'May I take a look at your passport please, sir?'

'Errr . . .' *Ha! Got him now!* He frowns.

'You do have one, don't you?'

'I . . . erm.' Stupid annoying showy-offy 8 and ¾ panics and pats his pockets furiously. His cousins and

Poppy and Hector are all seated one after the other on the slide. 8 and ¾ looks so flustered he stares at Poppy in blaming fury. 'DID YOU NOT PACK MY PASSPORT?' he roars at her.

'Don't blame me!' Poppy shrieks. 'I only met you five minutes ago.'

'You KNEW to pack the pass-ports!' he says, still locked in the improvisation game. 'That's your job!'

'I've already seen POPPY'S passport!' I lie. 'Didn't I, Poppy?'

'Yes.' Poppy sticks to the lie.

'I'm afraid anybody without a passport can't come to Egypt. Sorry about that.'

8 and ¾ looks at the bark on the ground, hoping he's dropped his imaginary passport *somewhere*, wishing for a leaf to fall, a chewing-gum wrapper to roll past, anything that will make a convincing prop as a passport, but I will not be convinced.

Losing at your own game is the worst.

And I can't help but smile and wave as we take our seats, buckle up for take-off and enjoy a safe and pleasurable slide/flight to the pyramids.

Chapter Nineteen

WEEK 5/6

'Darcy, it's for you . . .'

'Who is it?'

'A friend from school.'

Huh? I don't really have any friends from real-life school other than Will or . . . maybe there's Maggie, I guess, but she's on Girl Guide camp, making rope, eating beans out of tin pans and weeing in the bushes.

Still, I nearly break my neck tumbling down the stairs. 'COMING!' I shout.

It's Leila! Leila is my secret special friend from school who is basically a ninja mixed with a detective mixed with a superhero . . .

She's lying outside my new house with her hands behind her head, chewing on a blade of grass like an absolute boss. *Wow*. Why's she always got to be so good?

I'm wearing a Minnie Mouse vest top and spotty turquoise culottes and my hair is in bedraggled space bun knots on either side of my head. Meanwhile Leila absolutely eclipses me, again, with her mighty coolness.

'Writer's Bump!' (That's the cool nickname Leila gave to me when we met at the school sleepover. It's because of the funny bump on my finger that I got from writing so much.) She turns to me. She is wearing a camouflage two-piece. On me it would look like I was on my way to a fancy-dress party, but she wears it with red trainers and just looks great tbh. BLEUGH. BE SICK AT HER! Even the way she knows how to fold down her trainer socks so brilliantly at the back like an actual cool real person.

I don't bother asking her how she knows where I live. If you read my last writing book you would know that Leila just *pops* up wherever and whenever Leila feels like it. And Leila *always* knows. It wouldn't surprise me if she kidnapped the removal men or something.

'Did you want to hang out today?'

'Of course. Sure.' I don't hesitate to look like an absolute eager beast as per usual when it comes to Leila.

'Do you want to go to the forest?' Her eyes glint when she asks me.

'Yeah, but I have to ask my mum first,' I say, feeling all tumbling babyish, but it's a true real-life unavoidable fact.

''K. Go ask your mum,' she laughs. Out of her pocket she pulls a can of freezing cold Fanta and cracks it open with one hand and drinks it without her mouth touching the can. HOW *does she* DO *that?* WHO *even* HAS *a freezing cold Fanta just* SPARE *hanging around in their back pocket?*

'Gimme a sec.'

I dart into the house where Mum is arranging the under-the-stairs cupboard.

'Mum, can I go to the forest?'

'The forest?'

'Yes please.'

'What forest?'

'I don't know.'

'Well, go and find out.'

'Oh, but MUM!'

Mum is trying to jam the hoover in between these wobbly tins of paint and her patience is wearing awfully thin. I dash back outside. *Don't look* TOO *eager, Darcy! Hold it down.*

'Ready?' Leila asks me. Her long blonde hair unfolds like autumn leaves.

'Almost,' I lie. 'Which forest?'

'Just there.' Leila points into the distance where I can vaguely see some trees. That's enough evidence for me. I run back in to Mum.

She's right under the stairs now, her face all red and hot and puffy.

'It's just across the road, behind the houses.'

'No. I don't know it, so I'd rather you didn't, Darcy. You've got a whole new garden to play in outside.'

'BUT MUM, please, I'M SO BORED.'

'You always say it's impossible to be bored.'

'MUM! Can't you just LET me go?'

I get all tangled up and tight and stressed. I start to feel little fist balls clench either side of me and my teeth gritted up. My true Angrosaurus rex inside me wants to pour herself out and unleash but then a little tap at the door happens. It's Leila . . .

'Hello – Molly, is it?' Leila says to my mum *oh so cool and able to talk to mums* . . . and how does she remember her name? I DO NOT KNOW.

'Errr . . . yes . . . hello?' Mum tips back and pushes

her hair behind her ears like she's talking to a queen. *That's* the Leila effect.

'If there's a problem I've got a phone. You can take the number, but we are literally just going across the road.'

'Yes, I'll take your number, thank you . . . Sorry, I don't know your name?'

'It's Leila.' She winks at me when she says it and punches her number into Mum's phone.

I LOVE LEILA.

'OK, well, be back in a couple of hours, I want you

back for lunch, Darcy.' FOR LUNCH? Mum says it like it's an actual event, when we all know we just take turns to rummage in the fridge and see what's in date or hasn't already been taken or moan by Dad's side until he bothers to put some pasta on the boil.

'All right, Mum.'

And we are free. FREEEEEE . . . RUNNING in the warm toasty sun, our trainers beating down the tarmac street, happy and sunshine free and our shadows and dancing Peter Pan silhouettes with the puppet strings cut, all sharp and slanted and tall with spiky spider legs.

'Right,' Leila says, 'we have to climb this fence.'

OH NO. I HATE CLIMBING.

'No problem,' I lie.

'Is that a skirt you've got on? Be careful in case it gets caught on the spokes.'

'NO!' I grin. 'Culottes!' I stretch my legs out to show the shorts are attached, thinking that she might be that so impressed with my shorts/skirt that she might forget to break into the forest.

'Oh, cool! Just be careful you don't rip them when we climb.'

'OK.'

The fence is made up of big black iron railings with spokes. Scary and not allowed. And then I start to wonder why isn't there just a normal gate? I'm sure there is – it's just Leila, being *extra* as usual.

Then I watch her, with one hand, hurdle herself over the railings. And I am left. On the street. How do I even manipulate my body to get *up* something like this? Do I take a running jump? Do I throw myself at it and hope my body just snaps into place subconsciously and attacks the jump? Do I just run home?

No. Come on, if Leila did it with one hand you can do it with two.

'Come on, Writer's Bump!' She is already out of sight. What is she? A part-time squirrel?

What if I smash my teeth out?

And I just try and climb the painted shiny railings and my terrible trainers are just sliding off and my hands already hurt from tugging the spokes and I am using all my muscles but I can't . . .

'Here you go.' It's Leila, and she grabs her hands around mine and heaves me over. I can't help but smile when I remember that this was how we met, with her dragging me up by the hands. It's just as horrible the second time around. It hurts the entire time. *Ouch. Ouch.* YIKES! WAH! But I'm over.

'OK . . . what now?' I ask her.

'We be wild!' she says, and then she runs ahead. I follow her yellow-white hair swimming through and around the trunks like a flowing river, ribbons in a fan. 'Let's throw our shoes off!' she says and kicks her shoes off and chucks them behind her head. I do the same too, clumsily kicking them off at the heel.

It feels weird to have my feet all out in the bark and woods. At first it hurts to think about all the little jagged sticks and bits of twig and stone cutting the soles of my feet, but then I just have to get used to it and be a freed-up Amazonian wild beast.

Leila beats her mouth like a Native American. 'W-a-a-a-a—a-a-a-a—a-wa-a-a-a—a-a-a-a!' And I copy her too. I take my hair out all loose and let it fly . . . just like Leila. 'Climb a tree!' she says.

I gulp, but OK, I will, and I do, and I start using my hands and feet to jostle into all the peggy grooves and knots in the bark and clamber up. My legs scratch a bit and scuff, but I don't care as we climb up and up and up and up. Using our arms to wind and grip, to tangle and lift. I feel like an ape! Like the best monkey in the jungle!

'Shout anything!' Leila orders.

'Anything?'

'Yeah, anything . . .'

'ROOOOOOOAAAAARRRRRRR!' I shout.

'HA!' she laughs. 'That was good!'

'That's Angrosaurus rex.'

'Who is that?'

'She's my alter ego. She's the other side of me,' I explain.

'Sick! I wish I had an Angrosaurus rex,' Leila says. I sense she's impressed by me.

'Yeah, well, I've not been a very good friend to her. I've kept her locked up for a while.'

'Never mind. Well, let's unleash her!'

'I can't.'

'Why not?'

'I promised myself I wouldn't be dramatic this summer. It's a challenge our head of year gave us all.'

'Who's your head of year?'

'Mrs Hay.'

'Oh, that old handbag. She's like something from a black-and-white film. She's all right though.'

'Yeah, we have Mr Yates as our teacher . . . but not any more – that will be a shame, he's really nice.'

'Would he say you were dramatic?'

'Yes! I think everybody would.'

'Well, not me. I think your Angrosaurus rex isn't you being dramatic, Darcy, it's you being yourself!' She bends over the tree backwards, letting her long hair fly free. 'As long as you're not hurting anybody you're doing nothing wrong.'

And before we know it we are two rambling, wild, free Angrosaurus beasts, liberated in the forest. We roar and run and tumble. We shout and scream and sniff and be creatures. Our arms hang free, our fingers stretched out into the summer's day. Our feet are stomping and crashing! Elbows whacking, mouths open, faces scrunched up and tongues out like MMMUUUUAAAAHHHH!! We are set free in the wild where nothing matters. Where we don't have to answer to anything. With nature on our side. Where our shadows are monsters, with thorned spiked backs and ginormous teeth and jagged ears and terrifying claws!

GROWLING. HOWLING. PROWLING. SCOWLING.

RUUUUUUUOOOOOOOOOARRRRRR!

Until we pop out on the path. We find ourselves out of the foresty-type bit of the park and just on the actual path. And we are roaring in the face of a dog walker. Who jumps at us and then holds her chest. 'Ah, sorry, you made me jump,' she pants, all breathless.

'I was scared for a second. What am I like? Jumping at two little girls?'

'Sorry,' we mumble. 'We didn't mean to scare you.' We totter off with our heads held low in embarrassment. But sniggering and laughing, we begin to run. Smiles wrapped around our faces.

Leila turns to me and says, 'That was my best day of the holidays so far!'

And I want to say, 'Me too.' But I don't have to. I think that's evident in the way my cheeks ache from smiling and the new twinkle in my eye.

'That was quick!' Mum says, all surprised when I

walk in the door. I rush to the kitchen to get a drink, I am PARCHED. 'Did you have fun?'

'Yep,' I say in between furious gulps of squash.

'You look like you had a good run around,' Mum says.

I did. I ran around. And around. And around. Like the big Angrosaurus-rex child that I am.

And I feel so grateful. That I have a friend like Leila. Somebody that I don't have to see ALL the time, but whenever I do we can just pick up from where we left off. Where we can ramble to a place where, for once, no words are needed.

Chapter Twenty

WEEK 6/6

To Darcy,

Hi, Spain is so hot. Annie says you could crack an egg on the car bonnet and it would fry. I wanna try it, but she says we are not allowed. So boring. The road smells like wet tarmac. I've been swimming in the sea but I prefer the pool because the salt doesn't get in your eyes. I can do a backward roll in the water but sometimes the water gets up your nose. I have to be careful though because I sunburn because I'm ginger. Kids are allowed to stay up late here — it's cool, and you can have chocolate doughnuts for your breakfast if you want and nobody tells you off. You would love it. But I don't understand the Spanish TV. Are you OK?

Bye. From Will.

I flip the postcard round. It's of a sunshiny beach looking all so blissful and peaceful. I think it's quite rude that postcards don't come in envelopes. Not very private, are they? If I worked in a post office I'd be reading the backs of everybody's postcards all day. Like, I'd make it my main job. Be a brilliant way to spend your day.

And then I look up. As if by magic, his little freckly ginger sunburnt face is smushed up against the living-room window. Condensation puffing up against the glass and the print of his face. I scream in a delayed-reaction kind of way. Will! I run out to let him in. Lamb-Beth is pawing and circling his legs, and he scoops her up and props her over his shoulder.

'You're back!' I laugh.

'I am!'

'But I only just got your postcard.'

'Yeah, that's the thing about postcards.'

'I was worried about how to write you back so it's good you are here.'

'What would you write in the postcard back to me? What's new with you?'

'We've moved house and Donald has a really good operatic singing voice.'

'Your new house is well nice!' Will smiles, so impressed. 'And you, what you been doing?' he asks me, patting Lamb-Beth's back.

'Not much,' I flump. 'I've been sticking to my challenge though.'

'Really?' He laughs. 'What did you choose in the end?'

'Not to be dramatic.'

'Yeah, right! Ha-ha! Naaa! No way!'

'Yes way!'

'I just DO not believe for a second that you've kept that up.'

'YES I HAVE!' I feel my voice raise, but I have to hold it . . . but, OH MY GOD! I WANT TO ANGROSAURUS-REX SPLURGE MAD ALL

OVER EVERYWHERE AND PUNCH WILL
IN THE HEAD FOR DOUBTING ME AND
SHOUT AT HIM 'DO YOU HAVE ANY IDEA
HOW HARD THIS HAS BEEN FOR ME?
YOU HAVE NO RIGHT TO COME BARGING
BACK TO LONDON AND START TELLING
ME THAT I CAN'T DO SOMETHING!'
RRRRRUUUUUUUUOOOOOOOAAAA . . .

But for some weird reason, I don't. I just stay
calm and breathe deep. Being Angrosaurusy is SO
exhausting and childish and I am so passed that in my
older age.

'I have been very proud of myself, to be honest.
I've been really holding it together like an absolute,
actual pro,' I say.

'Whoa.' Will raises his brows. 'Normally you would
have shouted at me then. I am impressed,' he says.
'Can I see your room now?'

'Sure.'

We begin to climb up. Will lives in a small flat
with his sister Annie where everything is lovely and

close. I begin to get a bit nervous to show him my room because I don't want him to mention how high up and separate it is from everything else and draw attention to it being a bit scary, even though I'm much morer used to it that I once was. But suddenly, as we climb up the stairs, I begin to feel excited to show him my room, proud almost. I see the light coming down the way it always does, and its lovely woody treehouse smell, so familiar. So mine.

'WOW!' Will gawps. 'All this is yours?'

'Yeah,' I laugh. 'Do you like it?'

'Like it? I LOVE it!'

He looks around, and it feels like he's a hologram, like he's almost not really here. Like this beautiful bedroom isn't mine and how I've needed Will to be here to take it all in – mad how seeing somebody you love in a new space reassures you that it belongs to you and makes you feel safe.

'It's so sick – look at the beams, the wood, the view . . . bet you'll write some mad stuff up in here!'

I feel happy. Why does having the approval of someone mean so much more when it's come from someone you care about?

And just when we are about to go back down the staircase we see Lamb-Beth at the top of the stairs . . .

'Did you bring her up?' I ask Will.

'No. She just followed me up.' He smiles. 'Didn't you, Lamb-Beth?' He pats her softly on the head and she does a lamb purr. 'Is she allowed?'

'Yeah, course, it's just . . . she's never been able to do that before. The stairs were too steep. And she can now.'

'I think if your bedroom was in space, Darcy, she would find a way of getting up there!'

Before I know it . . . I can smell chocolate *everywhere* in the house. YUM! An afternoon treat!

'Oooo,' I sniff. 'What's going on?'

'Mum's making Mud Pie.' Poppy hurtles in, shrieking.

'What's Mud Pie?' I ask, running down to the kitchen. 'Smells delicious.'

'It's this new recipe I found in a magazine – doesn't it smell good?' Mum answers, leaning over a brown bowl.

'Yeah!' we all say, and Hector does this funny stupid chocolate dance.

'It will be ready soon, so why don't you guys go and watch TV for a bit while it cooks – it won't be made any quicker with you lot peering over my shoulder.'

We all go into the living room and pile up on the couch. I am so glad to have Will back. I have made him a friendship bracelet from Poppy's kit. It's orange and yellow with a brown thread running through it, but I don't want him to think it's anything to do with love so I probs might not give it to him just exactly right now.

'Would you rather lick a dog poo or every time you farted confetti blew out of your bum?' I ask Will.

'You're not allowed to say bum!' Poppy tells me off. 'I'll tell Mum!' Even though she says bum all the time, she's being annoying and winding me up for no real reason.

'Why not? It's a body part!'

'Confetti.' Will nods.

'Would you rather—'

'I don't want to play this game any more, it's so boring,' Hector decides even though he's not involved. 'Want to get trapped in the sofa bed?'

'Sure.'

We trap Will in the sofa bed and he obviously loves it and laughs his head off like a maniac, and so do we as we sit on top giggling.

'KIDS!' Dad shouts. 'MUD PIE!'

We all scramble clumsy wumsy through to the kitchen where all the Mud Pies are laid out. I can't tell you how delicious the whole smell is. I feel so excited to eat it. All gooey wooey chocolaty and comfort warmy in our tummy. Oh my, I could LIVE in this smell. I do a food dance – I can't help it.

All the bowls are fulled hugely to the top. White bowls loaded generously with the dark, dense, damp cake and the shiny sauce.

'Darcy, yours is that one,' Dad says, pointing to the big one at the end.

'My one? Why can't I just have *any* one?'

'Because . . . well . . . because you've been so good at your no-drama challenge we thought you deserved an EXTRA-LARGE portion!'

↑ DARCY

'NOT FAIR!' Poppy sulks.

'YEAH!' Hector joins in, folding his arms, grunting.

'It *is* fair. Darcy's done well.'

HAVE I? No, I HAVE! I HAVE DONE WELL!

Dad continues, 'You made a promise to yourself that you weren't going to be dramatic and you have stuck to it, which I know has been really hard. You've not been over the top about anything and we are proud of you. All those little silly things that would usually wind you up – you've just let them go. Well done.' Dad lifts his spoon, cheersing to me.

'HA!' YES, that's right! Extra-large portion for me! JEALOUS!

'Speech!' yells Will.

'Oh, all right!' I say, secretly LOVING that Will yelled 'SPEECH!' I've always wanted to give a round-the-table speech, you know. 'I mean, it wasn't easy,' I begin, like I'm collecting an award, 'but now I am a real hippy and I live a life of simplicity, peace and harmony. I am as quiet as the gentle breeze, floating like a feather, so chilled out like a deck-chair of a person . . . and I couldn't do this without the support of my own self and dedication to a goal. Thank you. You may eat!'

Everybody tucks in. I can see all their faces, melty

chocolate all tasty. I dip my spoon in. Mine doesn't look quite so nice and tasty up close. Still, pudding is allowed to look ugly – it's not about the presentation, it's about how it – *tastes* – *why does mine taste* – *all*—? *Wait a second* . . .

I scrunch my nose up, all disgusted. Everybody else is complimenting Mum about how yummy and scrumptious the Mud Pie is. Will has already nearly finished his bowl. Am I missing something? Mine is all coldish and grainy and earthy and soily and my mouth tastes all horrid, and when I look up Dad is laughing his head off. And just at that moment a big, fat, juicy, pink worm wriggles out of the 'Mud Pie'.

'Tricked you!' Dad laughs.

'You didn't?' Mum gasps in horror at him. 'What did you do?'

'I switched Darcy's Mud Pie for . . .' He can barely contain himself – he is laughing SO SO HARD he can't really string any words together. His face all creases up all squished, and he is laughing so hard he is snorting and wheezing and gone all red. 'ACTUAL MUD!' he shrieks.

Everybody gasps at me. Poppy. Hector. Mum. Will, and even Lamb-Beth, who has probably done a wee at one time on this mud.

'Your teeth are all muddy and black!' Hector shouts.

'Spit it out!'

'Gross!'

NO! I spit the fake cake out. All black dribble! I wipe my tongue. I jump up. Scratch my tongue. *Yuck! Yuck! Eugh!* NO! NO! 'Dad, HOW COULD

YOU?' Everybody begins to laugh. Not Mum – she is holding it back, too angry at Dad, I think.

'STOP laughing!' I screech. I rush to the sink and rinse out my mouth. Splatter water everywhere, and then Mum starts to laugh too. Even Mum.

'You HORRID mean dad, you don't even deserve to be a dad or have such a lovely precious thing as great as me to be your species of daughter, you absolute HORROR THING!' I yell. And now everybody is laughing so much. It's like the angrier I get, the harder they laugh.

'It was just a joke – there's a lovely big bowl there for you!'

But it's too late. I can't help it. It's like all the undrama of me has built up over the long days and turned me into a bottle of all-shooked-up fizzy drink and I am ready to just absolutely Angrosaurus-rex vex myself upon the WHOLE ENTIRE PLACE and thrash it all up to dust! HOW DARE HE EMBARRASS AND humili-ATE myself in front of MY family and best friend! Oh, HE WILL

REGRET this one, LET ME TELL YOU. I snort. I puff my cheeks out. I go white as a sheet first and then red. I feel myself burning up. Heart beating. Body tensing. My fists clench into balls. My toes roll up. My jaw clenches. My neck tightens. My shoulders stiffen. My brows frown. My face is ready to ROOOOOOAOAOAAAAAAARRRRRRRRR!

The Angrosaurus rex cannot stand it any longer. SHE IS READY TO SHOW HERSELF! Suddenly she becomes so mightily powerful and strong and is unable to hold it down any longer! Standing up on her hind legs, she tilts back, takes a big massive deep breath in and lets out the biggest scream of anger-madness-horror of the head-ruining, ripping, wrecking, rioting ROOOOOOOOOOOOAAAAAAARRRRRR!!!! She clambers through the forest, flinging trees back, springing them back so they snap behind her, the grass bending a path for her to stomp across. The birds flee from the trees. She scoops up the river and knots it into a bow, picks clouds out of the sky and pulls them into puffs like tearing out the stuffing of a teddy bear. STOMP! CRASH! ROOOOARRRR! Knocking down fences, scaring sheep, kicking mud, her claws raking the earth, her teeth gnashing, her tongue whipping, her eyes glaring. Her face screwed up into a tight, clenched ball.

'I think someone's tired,' Mum says.

'No, I am NOT!' I scream.

'Yes, you are. Come on, let's make you a nice cup of tea and you and Will can have a nice relax on the sofa.'

And Dad gets up. WHERE IS HE GOING NOW WHEN I AM CLEARLY RAGING AT HIM BUT—

'I DON'T WANT TO!' I shout at Mum.

'What has got into you, young lady?'

'What's got INTO me? WHAT'S got out of me, you mean – oh sorry, you must just mean my actual entire personality . . .' And everybody is suddenly shocked as I take a big deep breath in and open my mouth so wide and show my teeth, and I feel like they are big and oh so fanged, and I close my eyes and screwball up my face and my body all tense and I am ready to . . .

And then Dad comes back in, with a big beaming smile. The broadest biggest smile the world has ever seen, and behind him is Madison, from the workshop. She has her hair all in beautiful plaits and a lovely bright green top on with all her glorious bangles and she smells of woody things and flowers. And in her arms is the most wonderful thing I have ever evened seen.

'Oh my noodles!' Poppy shrieks. 'Darcy, you're a real writer now!' she gasps.

Because there, just for me, is the most amazing writing desk the whole world has ever seen.

'It's a writing desk – we made it for you at work.'

'But it's a no-reason present.' I am gobsmacked.

Madison shook her head and smiles. 'I don't think

so. When you came into the workshop that day and then got ill we all felt so sad – we loved having you guys in.'

'I knew I should have been employed full-time,' says Poppy (and she's absolutely correct by the way), but Madison continues, 'When your dad told us you were unwell and how you'd moved house and had been putting all this pressure on yourself to be "undramatic" we all felt so sorry for you! Your dad is a right drama queen for a boss!'

'That's true! And at home!' Mum laughed. 'Darcy – Dad and I have both been so amazed at how well you stuck to your challenge. So much has changed this summer and you've kept your cool pretty much the whole time. Five weeks ago we thought there was no way on this earth you'd stick to something like this. And it's not the NO-drama challenge specifically that we care about, it's that you've worked hard at something for yourself. What was a silly throwaway challenge at school has become a real achievement for you and we're very proud of you.'

'I'm sure you'll have lots of stories to tell after this experience . . . and you never know . . . if you continue to keep it up, we thought you might need somewhere to offload!' Dad joked.

'And so we made you this.' Madison smiled. 'We all did.'

'Even John Pincher with his bum on display?' Poppy giggled cheekily.

'Even John Pincher with his bum on display.' Madison cracked up. 'Well-ish, he ate a sausage roll next to me while I was cutting the wood once or twice,' she laughed.

'Come and see it then, D,' Dad says, and I realized I was so overwhelmed I hadn't even gotted up close to it.

But then I do. And I see the beautiful strong wood, the legs so sturdy and carefully varnished, not like any of the ugly desks at school. 'We put both Poppy and your puzzle designs on the top.' Dad points to the engravings. 'And a few other pieces . . .' He winks and I nearly cry to see little illustrations of all the wonderful beautiful special things that make me so happy. I look at Poppy and she nods, all cute and excited for me.

'Your mum drew most of them,' Dad says and looks at Mum who goes all shy.

'And me did one,' Hector butted in.

'They are to fuel your imagination. Or just to have around and inspire.'

Carved into the wood are little etchings of Lamb-Beth and my family. Of Will. Of my old house and my writing book. Of bugs and pancakes and animals and zombies and planets and stars and flowers and dragons and burgers and sweets and chocolate and monsters . . . and even my Angrosaurus rex.

'It's the SICKEST thing ever.' Will shakes his head in disbelief.

'Isn't it awesome?' Madison grins. 'Do you like it?'

'It's the most special thing in the world.'

'You did it, Darcy. If you can be not dramatic for five weeks, I reckon you can pretty much do anything!' Dad squeezes me tight and I hug him back. And Mum. And gingerbread-smelling Madison.

And I can only think to do one thing . . .

Cry my eyes out like the most dramatic sobby wobby corn on the cobby heart throbby baby that ever existed in the world. I cry harder than any actress in any film ever, and the more I seem to cry the more I seem to enjoy crying more. It's just such a relief to get it all out. And I hug everybody in the room and stroke my new fantastic desk over and over and throw myself across it, all strewn out like a dramatic actress, and everybody laughs and Mum says, 'Oh, she's back.' And that means me. That means my drama.

And I can't wait to go upstairs and write . . .

And write.

And write.

And write . . .

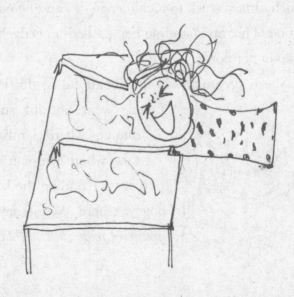

Chapter Twenty-One

WEEK 6/6 [END OF]

Darcy Burdock is daydreaming. She is dreaming of Mrs Hay learning that she VERY nearly...PRETTY much almost stuck to a challenge . . . and being very proud of her and handing her a rolled-up hedgehog to keep in her pocket.

She is dreaming about a beautiful world. Where

people wear hot-dog suits to dinner, where lambs can talk, where you can win a prize for finding the biggest bogey, where Wednesday is a *you must wear glitter all day* day.

Of music and sunshine. Of the smell of popcorn. Smiling faces. She is dreaming of the future. Of Poppy being a *growed-up* dancer, on stage, bowing to thousands of clapping people, fallen red roses by her feet, Mum and Dad crying their eyes out with pride, their hearts bursting out of their chests. She is dreaming of Hector directing horror films about zombie snakes – he has a chair with his own name on it. Will being a professional BMXer. Leila travelling the world being a karate kung-fu explorer. Donald Pincher, an actual real-life maybe friend of hers, is perhaps on a yacht of some kind, singing opera songs to the whales, and when he comes back from his travels they will go for ice cream. Timothy owns an elastic-band factory and is a ballet dancer. Madison makes desks for writing hippos. And John might wear some underpants?

It is beautiful in this place. In a world where nobody cares. Where everybody is happy.

And where is Darcy Burdock in the dream?

Oh, she is just here, in her writing room. Where she sits at a big grand desk covered in sparkly pens

and rainbow colours, where sunshine is pouring in through the window. She can see the big green trees outside and people of the world walking by. She is just finishing her latest book, *ANGROSAURUS REX*, a book inspired about herself when she was young.

When she has finished this last cup of tea, she will read the book back over to herself in a small whispery voice. If she is happy, she will send it to her publishers. They will make it into books and put the books on shelves and people will read it.

People like you.

Did you manage to decode the letter left for the new people in Darcy's old house?

DEAR WHOEVER LIVES HERE NEXT

Hello,

We are aliens from the future! You will NEVER be able to understand our special language unless you can speak the language of the future! Good luck trying to break the code!

The year is 3001! We are a family of genius aliens that lived in this house and every day we were sent on TOP-SECRET MISSIONS by our commander! Our names are Mum, Dad, Darcy, Poppy and Hector. We also have a pet lamb named Lamb-Beth.

Our favourite foods are magic space dust, cereal with gooey marshmallow martian lava syrup poured all over it. We also eat moon-cloud sandwiches, baked asteroid pasta bake, and milky-way cheesecake. It is very common here to eat dog poo. In fact if you do not TRY eating dog poo at least once, you will be in quite serious trouble: scientists have realized that dog poo is VERY GOOD for us! Make sure to say Hello to your new neighbours. They are aliens too! They eat LOTS of dog poo so it might be a nice idea to bake them a dog-poo cake? It is also very normal here to wipe your toothbrush in extra hot chilli sauce and eat fifty garlic cloves a day.

Other aliens will all be pretending to be humans so it is a very good idea to let them know you are an alien by doing a roly-poly right by their feet, licking their faces four times and doing a chicken dance. If that fails, then throw a freshly cooked fish pie over their heads, calling them a stupid idiot spoon raccoon-faced twiddleminch and farting really loudly in their right ear.

To fit in here nicely, run around the garden naked, paint your house rainbow coloured and act like EVERY DAY is YOUR birthday!

Good luck!

The Burdocks!

Acknowledgements

Thank you to my agents Jodie Hodges, Emily Talbot, Jane Willis and Dan Usztan. And all the team at United.

Thank you to my editor, Natalie Doherty.

Thank you to my copy editor, Sue Cook.

Thank you to the Design team at Penguin Random House, especially Dom Clements.

Thank you to all the libraries, schools, bookshops and reading groups that have supported Darcy.

Thank you to my readers. I love you. You're the best . . .

Thank you to my friends and family, especially my brother and sister for living this nonsense with me and to Fiona for putting up with it!

Hi Darcey (a different one with an E in her name)! Hi Beth! Hi Tegan! Hi Natalie! Hi Louis! Hi Angelo! Hi Georgie! Hi Lullah! Hi B! Hi Summer! Hi Nathaniel! Hi Dolly! Hi Charlie! Hi Jack! Hi Genie! Hi Lois! Hi Eva! Hi Lola! Hi Lacey!

And lots of love to all the Angrosauruses in the world. They are a thriving and amazing species.

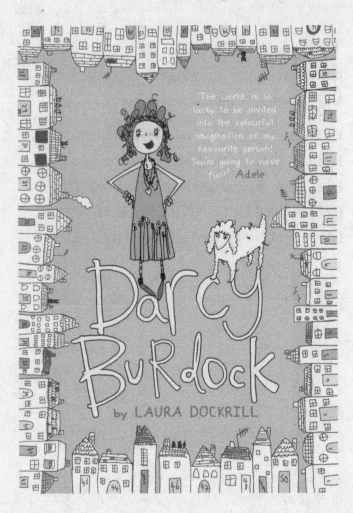

'The world is so lucky to be invited into the colourful imagination of my favourite person! You're going to have fun!' Adele

Darcy Burdock

by LAURA DOCKRILL

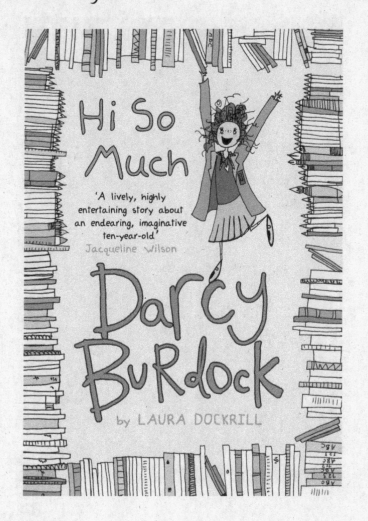

Hi So Much

'A lively, highly entertaining story about an endearing, imaginative ten-year-old'
Jacqueline Wilson

Darcy Burdock

by LAURA DOCKRILL

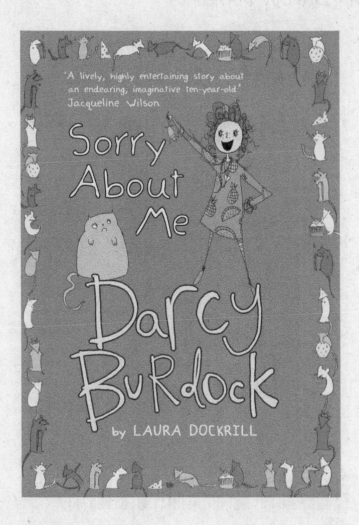

'A lively, highly entertaining story about an endearing, imaginative ten-year-old'
Jacqueline Wilson

Sorry
About
Me

Darcy
Burdock

by LAURA DOCKRILL

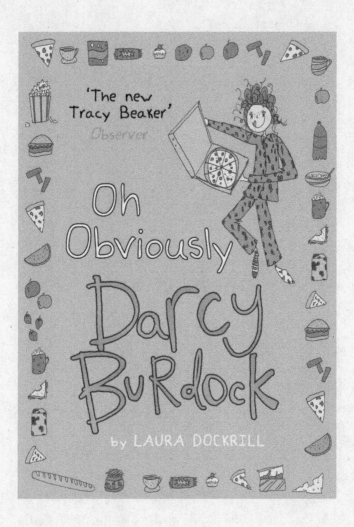

'The new Tracy Beaker'
Observer

Oh Obviously

Darcy Burdock

by LAURA DOCKRILL